AROUND

April: Seems the Connelly clan is full of surprises. The Chicago "royal family" just got bigger last week, when two long-lost illegitimate sons of Grant Connelly were welcomed into the fold. Wife Emma, ever the gracious hostess, held a party at their elaborate Lake Shore manor in honor of her new twin stepsons, Chance and Doug Barnett Connelly.

Grant may not have known of the twins' existence until weeks ago, but the newest Connelly men are upholding the family's noble traditions: Chance is a navy SEAL and Doug a respected Chicago doctor.

Rumor has it Chance is more than a bit uncomfortable in the concrete jungles of the Windy City, but is recuperating from a wound received on his last secret mission. That injury didn't keep him from putting the moves on Emma Connelly's social secretary, Jennifer Anderson, at the party last week. The spotlight-shy single mom was unavailable for comment—as would be yours truly, if over six feet of muscular male had set his sights in *this* direction!

The Connellys have been so much in the news these last few months that one can't help but wonder what other secrets the family could be hiding in their walk-in closets....

Dear Reader,

Welcome to Silhouette Desire, where you can spice up your April with six passionate, powerful and provocative romances!

Beloved author Diana Palmer delivers a great read with *A Man of Means,* the latest in her LONG, TALL TEXANS miniseries, as a saucy cook tames a hot-tempered cowboy with her biscuits. Then, enjoy reading how one woman's orderly life is turned upside down when she is wooed by *Mr. Temptation*, April's MAN OF THE MONTH and the first title in Cait London's hot new HEARTBREAKERS miniseries.

Reader favorite Maureen Child proves a naval hero is no match for a determined single mom in *The SEAL's Surrender,* the latest DYNASTIES: THE CONNELLYS title. And a reluctant widow gets a second chance at love in *Her Texan Tycoon* by Jan Hudson.

The drama continues in the TEXAS CATTLEMAN'S CLUB: THE LAST BACHELOR continuity series with *Tall, Dark...and Framed?* by Cathleen Galitz, when an attractive defense attorney falls head over heels for her client— a devastatingly handsome tycoon with a secret. And discover what a ranch foreman, a virgin and her protective brothers have in common in *One Wedding Night...* by Shirley Rogers.

Celebrate the season by pampering yourself with all six of these exciting new love stories.

Enjoy!

Joan Marlow Golan

Joan Marlow Golan
Senior Editor, Silhouette Desire

Please address questions and book requests to:
Silhouette Reader Service
U.S.: 3010 Walden Ave., P.O. Box 1325, Buffalo, NY 14269
Canadian: P.O. Box 609, Fort Erie, Ont. L2A 5X3

The SEAL's Surrender
MAUREEN CHILD

Silhouette
Desire

Published by Silhouette Books
America's Publisher of Contemporary Romance

Special thanks and acknowledgment are given
to Maureen Child for her contribution to
DYNASTIES: THE CONNELLYS series.

To Sandra Paul, Barbara Benedict, Angie Ray
and Michelle Thorne: Thank you for the ambush
and for my tiara. You guys are the best.

 SILHOUETTE BOOKS

ISBN 0-373-76431-6

THE SEAL'S SURRENDER

Visit Silhouette at www.eHarlequin.com

Printed in U.S.A.

Books by Maureen Child

Silhouette Desire

Have Bride, Need Groom #1059
The Surprise Christmas Bride #1112
Maternity Bride #1138
*The Littlest Marine #1167
*The Non-Commissioned Baby #1174
*The Oldest Living Married Virgin #1180
*Colonel Daddy #1211
*Mom in Waiting #1234
*Marine under the Mistletoe #1258
*The Daddy Salute #1275
*The Last Santini Virgin #1312
*The Next Santini Bride #1317
*Marooned with a Marine #1325
*Prince Charming in Dress Blues #1366
*His Baby! #1377
*Last Virgin in California #1398
Did You Say Twins?! #1408
The SEAL's Surrender #1431

*Bachelor Battalion

MAUREEN CHILD

was born and raised in Southern California and is the only person she knows who longs for an occasional change of season. She is delighted to be writing for Silhouette Books and is especially excited to be a part of the Desire line.

An avid reader, Maureen looks forward to those rare rainy California days when she can curl up and sink into a good book. Or two. When she isn't busy writing, she and her husband of twenty-five years like to travel, leaving their two grown children in charge of the neurotic golden retriever who is the *real* head of the household. Maureen is also an award-winning historical writer under the names of Kathleen Kane and Ann Carberry.

DYNASTIES: THE CONNELLYS

MEET THE CONNELLYS

Meet the Connellys of Chicago—
wealthy, powerful and rocked by scandal,
betrayal...and passion!

Who's Who in *THE SEAL'S SURRENDER*

Chance Barnett Connelly—If it weren't for his twin brother, this lone-wolf navy SEAL would never have tried to find his long-lost father, Grant Connelly. Chance had no idea what it was to be part of a family, especially the powerful, influential Connellys.

Jennifer Anderson—Ever since her husband was killed, she had been both a mother and a father to her baby girl. But meeting Chance made her long to remember what it had been like to be a woman....

Grant and Emma Connelly—True love allowed them to welcome home the twins from Grant's long-ago affair. But did their happiness blind them to a miscreant in their midst—one bent on seeking revenge on the Connellys?

One

He hated parties.

Give Chance Barnett a machine gun, and he was a happy man. Tell him to mingle, and you got a mean dog on a short leash.

But, Chance told himself, sometimes a man just had to bite the proverbial bullet. And this was a big one, in his humble opinion. Hell, it was damn near a mortar round.

He clutched his bottle of imported beer in a tight fist and made his way around the periphery of the party. His gaze narrowed slightly as he silently assessed his new family. A hell of a way to meet the relatives, he told himself, yet couldn't think of a better way to handle it.

There probably wasn't a *good* way to introduce him and his twin, Douglas, to the rest of the Connellys. Though to give them their due, they'd all taken the news of the twins' existence a lot easier than they might have. After all, it wasn't every day you met thirty-six-year-old illegitimate twin relatives, was it?

Though he had to admit that none of the Connellys had treated him and his brother as though they were somehow not good enough to be part of the family. Hell, even Miss Lily and Tobias had come home early from Palm Springs just to meet him and Douglas. Chance's gaze shot to the older couple. Correction, he told himself silently, his *grandparents*. Weird. He smiled as he watched Tobias trying to slip past his much smaller wife, but Miss Lily, cane or no cane, was too fast for her husband and snatched that glass of whiskey from his hand.

Interestingly enough, the big man just gave her a smile and a peck on the cheek. What would it be like, Chance wondered, to spend your life with one person? To love that one person so much that some fifty-odd years later, the stamp of it was still clearly on your features?

Those two old people had somehow managed to raise a dynasty. Amazing really, if you stopped to think about it. Sure, the Connellys were practically

American royalty. But they actually were *real* royalty as well.

And Chance and Douglas Barnett were a part of it.

He shook his head and moved on, drifting through the crowd like a finger of fog. A strident female voice caught his attention, and he slowed his steps, listening.

His half sister, Alexandra, a tall woman with raven-black hair, a too-important manner and sharp green eyes was center stage, where she seemed most comfortable. "I'm *so* sorry you won't have a chance to meet my fiancé," she was saying, "but Robert was called away on business."

Everyone in her audience nodded sagely, but all Chance could think was, Lucky guy. At least the missing Robert had gotten out of attending this party. He moved on, turning a bit too fast and feeling the pull of the stitches in his side.

A reminder of the reason he was able to be here at this party. If he hadn't been wounded on his last mission, he'd have been happily out trooping through a jungle somewhere. And as soon as he was healed enough, that was just what he'd be doing. Hell, he kept his duffel bag packed and ready to go.

Man, was he ready to go. He needed to get back to his SEAL team. Needed to get back where he belonged. He scowled to himself. He caught a glimpse of Doug, chatting it up with a few of their new relatives, and almost wished that he was half as at ease with people as his brother. Hell, he'd even heard his twin talking to one of their new cousins about his ex-wife and how the reason they'd broken up was because she hadn't wanted the children Doug wanted so badly. Yeah. Chance's brother was sliding right into this and didn't seem to have any trouble at all stringing the name *Connelly* behind the Barnett they'd grown up with. But then, Doug always had been the reasonable twin. Which was probably why Chance had grown up to be a fighting man and Doug had become a doctor.

Okay, he thought, way too philosophical.

"Excuse me, sir." A low-pitched voice came from right behind him and Chance spun around to face a tuxedo-clad waiter. "May I get you something from the bar?"

Chance held his beer aloft. "No thanks," he said, shaking his head at the realization that these people probably dealt with in-house waiters and butlers all the time. "I'm covered."

Maybe it was the military training and maybe it was just his own innate need to be in control at all times, but Chance rarely had more than one beer at a party. Even one like this, where he felt more out of place than a pauper in a palace.

The waiter moved off soundlessly into the milling crowd and Chance shook his head again. How had he wound up here? he wondered. And just how soon could he make a polite exit? He moved off into a corner of the room, kept his back to the wall and let his gaze slide across the people filling the cavernous room.

A SEAL in a Lake Shore mansion? He chuckled inwardly at the absurdity of it. Hell, nobody would buy that. He stood out from the elegantly dressed crowd. His U.S. Navy whites were startling in a sea of bright colors and black tuxedos. But for the first time in his life, he was also in a room filled with people he was actually related to.

He and Douglas had grown up alone, raised by a single mom who'd done her best. But she hadn't been able to provide enough of her own presence to satisfy her boys—let alone provide relatives. So here he stood, a thirty-six-year-old man suddenly meeting cousins and half brothers and sisters for the first time.

Weird.

He took a sip of beer, swallowed it and silently admitted that family wasn't necessarily a bad thing. It was just going to take some getting used to. From across the room, Douglas caught his eye and gave him a "Do you believe this?" look and a half smile. Instantly, Chance felt more at ease. He and his twin had pulled each other through plenty of scrapes over the years. And as long as they could count on each other, then tacking the name *Connelly* on after the Barnett wouldn't change much.

Still, he could do with some air.

Instinctively, he moved toward the sliding glass doors that led onto a balcony. The muted noise of conversation and softly-played piano music followed him as he skirted the crowd. But as he neared the glass partition, his plan for solitude fell apart.

A woman stood on the balcony in the late-afternoon sun, her short, light-blond hair tousled by the wind. He knew her. Jennifer Anderson, Emma Connelly's social secretary. They'd met a couple of times in the last few days. She wasn't very tall, but every inch of her looked to be packed to perfection. She wore a deep-green dress with a flippy sort of hem that stopped just short of her knees, displaying to their best advantage what looked to be excellent legs. Her breasts were high and full and her waist was narrow enough that he figured given a chance, he could span that distance with both hands. Her back was straight as she stared out at Lake Michigan, but he frowned as he noticed she kept one hand clapped across her mouth and couldn't quite hide the droop in her shoulders.

Instantly, something inside him stirred to life. The protective instinct was strong and he felt it push him outside. He slid the glass door open, and the wind off the lake tried to shove him back into the party. But SEALs didn't give up that easily.

Chance ducked his head, stepped quietly onto the stone balcony and soundlessly closed the door behind him.

"Get a grip, Jen," the woman muttered to herself before he had a chance to announce his presence. "Crying's not going to help. It's only going to make you look like hell."

Well, he couldn't resist responding to that.

"Lady," he said softly, "all the tears in the world would have a hard time pulling that one off."

She turned quickly, her body language letting him know that she wasn't pleased at having been found giving in to tears. But she recognized him right away and the Keep Out sign in her eyes blinked off.

"You surprised me," she said, lifting one hand to swipe away the telltale track of tears on her cheeks.

"Sorry," he said, though he really wasn't. "Old habits. I'm used to moving quietly."

One blond eyebrow lifted into an arch. "This isn't exactly the jungle, Commander," she said. "Around here, most people knock."

"Ah," he said, walking closer, "but you knock when you want to come *in*. I was coming *out*."

"Great," she muttered thickly, turning her face back into the wind. "Semantics."

Jennifer stared out at the horizon, deliberately ignoring him in the hopes that he'd go away. She couldn't very well *order* him off. Not one of the long-lost sons for whom this party had been arranged. So either he left of his own accord, or she'd be forced to go back to the party and pretend everything was all right.

Please God, let him leave.

Apparently though, God wasn't listening.

Chance Barnett Connelly moved up right beside her and curled his hands over the wrought-iron balcony railing. She glanced down at those strong, tanned hands and noticed that his knuckles whitened with his grip. Obviously, he felt as tense as she did. But their reasons, at least, were very different.

"So," he said, keeping his gaze locked on the wall of clouds hanging just at the horizon, "what seems to be the problem?"

"Problem?" She straightened up. The last thing she wanted or needed was sympathy. Especially from a man she didn't even know. Besides, he was a Connelly. If she told him, then soon everyone would know and she'd like to put that off for as long as she could. At least until she'd had a chance to talk to Emma Connelly first.

Along with being her boss, Emma was as close to a mother figure as Jennifer could claim. Her own parents had died years ago, and but for her daughter, Sarah, Jennifer was alone in the world. Which had never really bothered her. Until yesterday.

"Yeah," Chance said, shifting her a glance, "when I see a beautiful woman alone and crying on a balcony while there's a party going on not five feet from her...well, I naturally figure there's a problem."

She inhaled sharply, taking the cold wind inside her, needing the bracing strength of it. Then, she forced a cheer she didn't feel into her voice. "Thanks for asking, but I'm fine. Really."

"Uh-huh."

"I mean it."

"Yeah, I can see that."

She looked at him from the corner of her eye. "But you don't believe me."

"Nope."

"Well," she said, pushing away from the balcony railing, "that's not my problem, is it?"

He reached out and grabbed her forearm. "Don't go."

His touch felt warm and strong and seemed to wrap itself not only around her arm, but around her bruised heart, too. Jennifer stopped short and lifted her gaze to look into amber eyes the exact color of fine, aged brandy. Her heartbeat stuttered slightly. His jaw looked as though it had been carved of granite. His nose had obviously been broken at least once sometime in the past. His brown hair was military-short, but even at that, there was a slight wave to it that made a woman want to stroke her fingers through it.

And good Lord, he was tall. With shoulders broad enough to balance the world. Today she could surely use a pair of shoulders broad enough to lean on. But Jennifer was too used to standing on her own two feet to take advantage of a near stranger in a weak moment.

As if he could read her mind though, he said, "I didn't mean to intrude, but now that I'm here, why not let me help if I can?"

Tempting, she thought. Oh, so tempting. But no. She shook her head. "I appreciate it, but—"

"I'm a stranger."

"Well," she said, "yes."

"Sometimes that's better." He kept his grip on her forearm as if he expected her to scurry for the door. Which she would have done, given half a chance. Then he smiled and her stomach flipped over. "Telling your troubles to a stranger is like talking to yourself. Only you don't have to answer your own questions and run the risk of being locked in a padded room."

A return smile tickled the corners of her mouth and she had to fight to keep it from blossoming. Which was a good thing actually, since she hadn't had a thing to smile about since talking to her daughter's doctors yesterday. And that stray thought was enough to wipe the beginnings of humor from her face.

A cold, empty well opened up inside her and she felt her heart slide into it.

"Hey," he said, letting his hand slide from her forearm up to her shoulder, where his fingers squeezed gently. "Come on. Talk to me. Maybe I can help." He dipped his head a bit and gave her another half smile. "I'm a SEAL. Trained to be a hero. So let me ride to the rescue here, okay?"

Jennifer glanced over her shoulder at the party just beyond the glass doors, then turned back to look at him again. What the heck, she thought. She *could* use a shoulder at the moment. And his were certainly broad enough to hold up under her assault.

"It's my daughter," she blurted before she could change her mind.

His gaze darkened slightly. "You have a daughter?"

"Yes." Just the thought of Sarah brought up her image in Jennifer's mind and she smiled to herself. Big brown eyes in a round little face that was usually smudged with dirt. Pigtails that were really no more than tiny wisps of light-brown hair caught up in barrettes at either side of her head. Small, pudgy hands and short, sturdy legs. Butterfly kisses and sticky-fingered hugs. Tickle bugs and belly laughs.

Doctors in white coats, long, dangerous-looking needles and Sarah's tears.

"Oh, God," Jennifer half moaned and clapped her hand to her mouth again, not sure if she was going to be sick or start screaming.

It was all just so damned unfair.

"Come here," Chance said, turning her as he spoke, shifting to hold her, wrap his arms around her.

And because she needed a hug so badly, she went.

Nestled against that wide chest, she hung on for a long moment, wrapping her arms around his waist and drawing on the strength he so casually offered. She felt him awkwardly patting her back and for some silly reason, it helped. Though she knew it didn't actually change anything, the physical act of being comforted soothed the frayed edges of her soul, and just for an instant, the world didn't seem as terrifying as it had only minutes ago.

"Tell me," he said, his voice a gruff whisper coming from somewhere above her head. "Tell me what's wrong."

"Sarah," she said, saying the words aloud for the first time since the doctor had so clinically outlined the trouble the day before, "my baby. She needs an operation. On her heart. There's a small hole in it."

"Aah..." A comforting sound, more of a deep breath released, maybe, but it too helped. She felt his sympathy in the gentle tightening of his grip on her. "How old is she?"

"Eighteen months," she whispered, looking past him to the lake, but really looking at her mind's-eye picture of Sarah. "She's so small. So tiny. This shouldn't be happening."

"No, it shouldn't," he said softly. "It sucks."

Jennifer nodded. "Yes," she said, grateful to hear someone else say what she'd been thinking, "it does."

Two

Chance wasn't a family kind of man by any means. But he felt Jennifer's fear as if it were his own. It rattled through her small body with the force of a freight train and shook him to his bones.

His every instinct told him to rush in and defend. Protect. But none of his training would do a damn sight of good here. And that realization was a bitter pill to choke down.

Hell, he couldn't even think of something helpful to say. It sucks? Real eloquent, Chance.

He continued to hold her though, hoping his silent support helped in some way. Strange, a few days ago, he hadn't known or cared that any of these people existed. Now he was standing on the balcony of a *mansion,* for Pete's sake, holding a weeping woman.

"What am I doing?" Jennifer muttered as she pulled back out of his arms and took another step away from him just for good measure. "I'm going to rain mascara all over your white uniform."

No she wouldn't, he thought, looking into those forest-green eyes of hers. They were big and wet and sad, but there was no smudge of dark makeup around them. Just the remnants of tears she was fighting to control. Damned if he didn't admire her for that, too.

She could be wallowing in the fear that was close to strangling her, but she wasn't. Instead, she was holding herself together through the force of her will. Hell, she didn't even want sympathy. So what exactly was it he could do for her?

"Do you want to go back inside?" he asked.

"God no," she said, shaking her head and moving back to the railing. Keeping her face averted from both him and the sliding glass doors behind them, she said, "I don't want them to know I've been crying. I just couldn't take the questions right now."

Privacy. Something else he could understand. Well, if he couldn't escort her through the maze of party-goers, he could at least make her eventual trip inside a little easier. "Okay. Just wait here, then. I'll be back."

Before she could say anything, he opened the sliding glass doors and stepped back into the party. Noise assaulted him and he instantly missed the relative peace and quiet of the balcony.

Focused, Chance paid no attention to the people around him. He moved through the crowd as if he were on a mission. He kept his goal in mind and went about accomplishing it as quickly as he could. Which wasn't as easy as he'd expected. There were just too many people.

He cast one quick, nearly wistful glance at the front door, then forgot about leaving and went on with his quest.

When he walked into the kitchen, the folks in there looked as surprised as they would have if lightning had struck the butcher-block work island in the center of the massive room.

"Can I help you, Mr. Chance?"

Grateful, he looked to the woman on his right. Mentally, he scrambled for her name and came up with it an instant later.

"Ruby, right?" he asked.

"That's me," the housekeeper said, giving him a nod sharp enough to shake loose a graying red curl from her topknot to lie askew in the middle of her forehead.

In the few days he'd been in town, Chance had

seen this woman running the Connelly household—
and family, for that matter—with an iron fist. Grant
and Emma might think they were in charge, but the
truth was, Ruby was the brass around here.

The short, slightly rounded woman with kind
blue eyes had the ability to get things done, and
Chance appreciated that. Even while keeping under
radar, staying unnoticed himself. He'd seen how his
half brothers and sisters scampered when Ruby
gave an order. Hell, even his father, Grant, didn't
argue when she laid down the law.

Clearly, she'd been in charge so long, she never
even considered the possibility that people wouldn't
obey her without question. In the military, she
might have made it to the Joint Chiefs of Staff.
Here, she ran the Connelly household like a well-
oiled machine and wouldn't accept anything less.

"Now, how can I help you?" she asked, snatching his attention as she would have the hand of a
child inclined to wander off.

Chance glanced around at the others clustered
within hearing distance, reluctant to speak up with
so many eager ears nearby. The housekeeper noticed and clapped her hands sharply. "What are you
bunch staring at? Get about your business. Don't
you have drinks and canapés you could be serv-
ing?"

They scattered like windblown leaves, and, in

seconds, he was alone in the room with Ruby. "I'm impressed," he said.

"For running them off? Don't be. I am sorry about them, though," the woman said, with a shake of her head. "They're day help for the party and their mamas apparently forgot to teach them any manners."

He smiled. "I have a feeling you'll take care of that."

She straightened up and puffed out her chest. "I'll do my best in the short time I have them," she assured him. "So what is it you need, Mr. Chance?"

He winced a little at the implied title. Now, people calling him "Commander," he'd earned. He could even live with "Hey, sailor," but "Mr. Chance"? No way. That was just way too highfalutin. "Just, Chance, all right?"

One corner of her mouth twitched, but she only nodded. "Chance it is, then." She studied him for a long minute, then said, "You know, you've the look of your father around the eyes. More so than your brother does."

Chance shifted uncomfortably. He didn't necessarily want to be reminded that he looked like the man who'd managed to ignore both him and his brother their whole lives. What was he supposed to say to that, anyway? Thank you didn't seem appropriate somehow. So he ignored the comment entirely.

After all, it wasn't as if he'd come here looking to find family. He already had his family. Douglas. With the death of their mother, all they had left was each other. And that had always been enough before.

The only reason he was here at all was as a favor to Doug. And if he hadn't been shot by that sneaky little terrorist on his last mission, he wouldn't have had to put up with any of the pomp and circumstance surrounding the Connellys. But then, he wouldn't have been here to ride to Jennifer's rescue, either, would he?

And that thought returned him to why he'd come to the kitchen in the first place.

"Any chance I could get a glass of water and a box of tissues?" he asked.

Ruby narrowed her eyes thoughtfully as she looked at him. "Feel a crying jag coming on, do you?"

Chance played along. "Yes, ma'am. I'm feeling real emotional."

She snorted. "Yeah, I can see that." But without another word, she bustled around the room and came back with just what he'd asked for. As he turned to leave the room, though, her voice stopped him. "You tell Jennifer for me that everything's going to be all right."

He looked at her. Shouldn't be surprised, he thought. He'd already discovered that nothing much went on around here that Ruby didn't know about. "What?"

"I've been with the Connellys for more years than I care to admit. Not much gets past me. I know there's something wrong."

Nodding, he told her, "You would have made a good admiral."

"Phooey," she said, waving one hand to dismiss him. "Admirals are small stuff. I'd have made a good president."

"You know something?" he said, giving her a wink, "I believe you." Then he slipped from the room before she could give him any orders he'd be too afraid not to follow.

"Oh, this is good," Jennifer told herself aloud as she clutched the balcony railing and stared out at Lake Michigan. "Way to ensure your employment, Jen." Shaking her head, she blinked back tears that still threatened and solemnly vowed they wouldn't fall. She'd already screwed up big-time.

What had she been thinking? Crying on the shoulder of the guest of honor at her employer's party. The one time she indulged in a good old-fashioned pity party, she had to be caught by Mr. Tall, Dark and Dangerous.

"For goodness' sake," she grumbled, tightening

her grip on the cold iron railing. She lifted her face into the wind sweeping in off the lake and told herself that if she was very lucky, the newest addition to the Connelly family would keep her embarrassing behavior to himself.

Although, for all she knew he was inside now, trying to get Emma to come out and comfort her, readily handing off the crazed secretary to someone else. She could almost imagine him, stalking through the party, heading for the front door as fast as he could. And she couldn't really blame him, either.

What man wanted to be a human tissue for a weeping woman? Especially one he hardly knew.

Behind her, the glass door slid open, allowing a brief pulse of conversation and piano music onto the balcony, and in an instant, the door closed again, sealing off the intrusion.

She didn't turn around. She didn't have to. She knew who it was. She *felt* his presence almost as an electrical charge. Her nerve endings hummed and the hairs at the back of her neck stood straight up.

Probably not a good sign.

"Sorry I took so long," he said and darned if his voice didn't scrape along those already tense nerves.

Get a grip, Jen. He's your boss's stepson. He's a stranger. He doesn't give a damn about your problems and there's nothing between you but an embarrassing crying jag.

So why was her stomach suddenly in knots and her breath coming fast and hard?

Because you're an idiot, she told herself just before turning to look at him.

Well, that didn't help any. He was just too darned good-looking, that was the problem. He looked like a poster boy for navy recruiting. Or like one of those navy lawyers on that television show. His uniform shone a bright white against the backdrop of the blue lake and shimmering April sky. The ribbons decorating his chest drew her eye as did the SEAL pin he wore proudly. Then she looked farther up, into his eyes, and saw...concern. And that nearly did her in on the spot.

Darn it.

"You okay?" he asked.

"Oh, dandy," she told him and sniffed.

He held out the box of tissues and she gratefully snatched one free of the dispenser. She wiped her eyes, blew her nose and still didn't feel better.

"Here, drink this." He offered the tall, pale-blue glass he carried.

"What is it?" she asked as she reached for it. "Hemlock?"

"Nothing so deadly," he said with a half laugh. "Just water."

She took a drink, letting the liquid soothe her

tight throat before trying to talk again. Lifting her gaze to his, she said, "Thank you. For the tissue and the water."

"Here to serve, ma'am," he said.

"But I bet you didn't expect to have to go above and beyond the call at a party."

He shrugged. "Hey, a party, a terrorist situation—the SEALS can handle it all."

"Good to know," she muttered, then, still clutching her glass of water, turned around again to stare out at the lake. She couldn't keep looking at him. That just wasn't good for her equilibrium. Way better on her nerves to stare out at a lake the size of an ocean, its choppy waves slapping toward Lake Shore Drive.

"Tell me about your daughter," he said quietly and Jennifer's eyes closed briefly on a twinge of something as painful as it was tender.

But she supposed she owed him this, for crying all over him.

"Sarah's so smart," she said, and though her voice started out thin and trembling, talking about her pride and joy strengthened it. Shaking her head, she continued, "She started talking before she was a year old and now she's already arguing with me." Jennifer chuckled, and the sound grated against her throat. "When she's a teenager—" *when* not *if,* she told herself silently "—we'll probably lock horns all the time."

"Probably," he said agreeably. "God knows Doug and I drove our poor mother nuts when we were teenagers. Of course your Sarah most likely won't be into drag racing, so that's one worry you won't have."

She flicked him a glance, not at all surprised by his little admission. He was a SEAL, after all. And clearly he loved his job. So it naturally followed that as a kid, he would have sought out dangerous pastimes.

Just like Mike, she thought with an inward acknowledgment of old pain. The two of them would have gotten along great together, no doubt. Then, as if he'd sensed what she was thinking, the man beside her spoke up again.

"Your husband must be just as proud of her as you are," Chance said.

"My husband's dead," she said, tasting the words it had taken her so long to get used to saying.

"Oh. I'm sorry," he said.

"You didn't know," she said softly. "No reason to be sorry. He's been gone almost two years now." She sighed heavily. "He never even knew Sarah."

A long uncomfortable minute passed before he said, "I was raised by a single mother," he said. "I know how hard it is."

She looked up at him, into those whiskey-colored eyes and read understanding there. And darn it, she appreciated it. Though Emma was beyond kind and a good friend as well as an employer, she couldn't really appreciate what it was like to be the sole person responsible for raising a child. Not when she had Grant, as much in love with her today as he had been years ago.

Then he said, "If you don't mind my asking, how did your husband die?"

"Mike was a police officer," she said, lifting her chin just a bit. "He was killed in the line of duty. I was still pregnant with Sarah when he died. He never even *saw* her."

"Maybe he did," Chance said and she looked at him. "Maybe he sees her every day."

"I'd like to think so."

"I've seen enough things over the years to convince me that anything's possible." He paused for a long minute, then said, "I never knew my father, either." Then he stopped and laughed shortly. "At least, not until a few days ago."

She shook her head in sympathy, though she was glad to turn the subject away from Mike. "I can't even imagine what that must be like," she said, choosing her words carefully now. "Finding your blood father after so many years..."

He nodded, lifting his face into the cold, sharp wind. "I know what you mean. I'm not real sure how I feel about it, either. But," he said, giving a quick look over his shoulder, "it meant something to Doug, so here I am."

"You only came here for your brother's sake?"

"Why else?"

"To get to know your family?"

"Nah. My mother's gone now, so my family is Doug. The rest..." He shook his head again as if he didn't know quite what else to say.

"The Connellys are nice people," Jennifer said, wanting him to know that this new family of his was ready and willing to welcome him.

"Seem to be."

"They've been wonderful to me and Sarah."

He gave her a slow smile. "If your daughter's anything like you, I can't see that that would be a hardship."

Oh, that smile was just as dangerous as the man, she told herself, taking a mental step backward. She didn't need this kind of complication right now. Her world was Sarah. Her attentions had to be devoted to making her little girl well again. And to help her keep her attentions focused, she knew the best thing to do was to keep her distance from this man.

"I, uh—" She glanced at the sliding glass doors with real regret. Though she knew she had to leave the balcony, she wasn't looking forward to making small talk while her heart was aching. Still, this party was a big deal for Grant and Emma. Hadn't Jennifer and her employer been planning it for weeks? No, heartache or not, she had to do her job.

"I'd better get back inside," she said and even she heard the reluctance in her voice.

Chance straightened away from the railing and looked from the doors to her. She wasn't ready to go back in there and face the chattering mob. He could see it in her eyes. The vulnerability was still there, etched deep.

It was none of his business, of course, but still, he felt a kinship of sorts with her. She was a single mother, as his own mom had been. Her husband had served the public, his country, as Chance did, only *he* had paid the ultimate price. A rising wave of protectiveness filled him and before he could think more of it, he said, "I think the party can get along without either of us. So why don't you let me take you home instead?"

She thought about it for a long minute, and he could see in her eyes just how much she wanted to get out of here. The question was, would she?

"As much as I'd like to," she said, "I don't think I should—"

"With that crowd in there, no one will even miss us."

"Emma would."

He acknowledged that with a brief nod. "Okay, then, we'll stop and tell her we're leaving. I should say thanks, anyway."

Now that her objections were taken care of, all that was stopping her from taking him up on his offer was the fact that he was a virtual stranger— long-lost relative of her employer or not. "You can trust me," he said softly.

Her lips twitched slightly. "It's not that," she said.

"Then what? I'm just offering you a ride home, not a weekend trip to Jamaica." Why was he trying so hard to convince her? He wasn't sure. All he knew was that suddenly he needed to be the one to see her safely to her door.

She looked beyond the glass doors again to the party, and he saw her shudder. She really didn't want to go back in there. And damned if he could blame her. He had no interest in rejoining the mob, either.

And playing on that feeling, he said, "You'd be doing me a favor."

"What?"

He smiled. "You'd be rescuing me from mingling."

Her lips twitched. "A fate worse than death?"

"Oh, definitely."

She nodded, and he knew this battle was won. "Well," she said, her decision made, "I suppose I shouldn't turn down my one chance to be a hero."

Three

A thick wall of noise welcomed them back inside the Connelly mansion, and for one brief moment, Jennifer thought about turning tail and disappearing again onto the balcony. But it wouldn't do any good. She had to make it through the minefield of the party to make good her escape at some point anyway. Better to do it now, when she had a tall, imposing man striding beside her, subtly clearing a path.

Faces flashed past as Chance steered her through the crowd with one strong hand at the small of her back. His touch felt warm, comforting, somehow. Strange, but she hadn't experienced that little nicety since Mike's death and she hadn't realized how much she had missed it. But then, she'd realized over the last couple of years that it was the small things that, once they were gone, left the biggest holes.

Now there was no one to hold her chair out for her at a nice restaurant. No one who knew how to whistle for a cab loudly enough to gather up a regular cluster of them. No one to kill a spider in the bathroom in the middle of the night. No one to warm her feet on, or to whisper to in the movies. No one to care for, to cook for, to worry about.

A wistful smile crossed her face. Of course, any self-respecting women's libber would have a heart attack if she could read Jennifer's mind. But she didn't care. She had always considered herself pretty liberated, but when it came right down to it, she'd *liked* being married. She'd *liked* being half of a team. And sometimes she missed that feeling so much, a slow, deep ache wrapped itself around her heart.

But then all it would take was one sweet smile from Sarah and everything was all right again. Silently, she reminded herself that she would never be alone again, not really. Not as long as she and Sarah had each other.

And that thought made her think of the heart operation her baby needed, and tears welled up in her eyes. It didn't seem to make a difference that the doctors all assured her that it would be a simple thing, as operations went. That though any procedure carried risks, Sarah had an excellent chance at a full and complete recovery.

Because no matter the kind words and assurances, Sarah was her baby. Her family. And the thought of losing her was simply too much to contemplate. She couldn't even imagine a world without her little girl in it—so she didn't. Jennifer blinked frantically, slammed a mental door on the dark, worrisome thoughts and hurried her steps. All she wanted now was to get out of here before she could be bombarded with concerned questions.

"There they are," Chance muttered, bending his head close to her ear.

Her gaze shifted to the right and she saw Grant and Emma Connelly, having what looked to be a very involved discussion with Seth. None of them looked very happy.

Jennifer slowed down instinctively, not wanting to intrude on what was obviously a strained moment. Shaking her head, she shot a glance up at the man beside her. "It looks like they're busy. Maybe we shouldn't interrupt."

He took her upper arm in a firm, but gentle grip and gave her a smile. "We won't interrupt them for long. Then they can go back to whatever it is that's got them all frowning so."

As they approached the threesome, Jennifer overheard Seth saying, "I just have to go and see her. I don't want to hurt you, Mom," he said to Emma, "but Angie Donahue is my birth mother. And I have to know why she suddenly wants to see me." He reached for Emma's hand and gave it a squeeze. "I'll be fine. I promise. And I'll be back."

Through teary eyes, Emma glanced at Grant, who kept his gaze focused on the young man in front of him, as though, if he studied him hard enough, he'd be able to pull the thoughts from Seth's mind. Finally, though, the elder Connelly said gruffly, "You do what you have to do, son. We're behind you all the way. Just like always. And we'll be here waiting for you when you come home."

Whatever the boy might have said in response was lost when Emma noticed Chance and Jennifer approaching. She smiled in welcome and made shooing gestures at Seth with both hands.

"And what are you two up to?" she asked as they came closer.

"I just wanted to say thank you, ma'am, for your hospitality," Chance said, then added, "and to say goodbye."

"Goodbye?" Grant asked abruptly. "Already?"

Jennifer's gaze flicked from father to son and though she knew Chance probably wouldn't be happy to hear it, she privately acknowledged just how much he looked like his biological father. But it wasn't just their features they shared. Both of the men had an air of self-confidence about them that people naturally gravitated toward.

It was part of the reason Grant had done so well in the business world—and why Chance would inevitably continue his rise through the ranks. No doubt one day he'd be an admiral. Men like the Connellys were born conquerors. All that differed were the prizes they sought.

"Jennifer's not feeling well," Chance was saying, "so I offered to take her home."

"Aah…" Grant nodded thoughtfully as his gaze flicked from his son to Jennifer and back again.

Jennifer felt her cheeks warm up at the knowing gleam in Grant's eyes, so she spoke up quickly. "I, uh—" think fast, Jen "—have a headache," she finished. Well, that was brilliant. But she didn't want to go into Sarah's medical problems now. Not at the party. "Commander Barnett was kind enough to offer me a ride."

"Barnett?" Grant stared at the man who was his son.

A touchy subject, Jennifer knew. Chance quite naturally wanted to keep the name he knew. The name his mother had given him. Grant, just as naturally, wanted his sons to use his name.

It would be interesting to see who eventually won this little tug-of-war.

"Sir," Chance said, holding his right hand out to his father, "thank you. It was a nice party."

Grant harrumphed. "You hated it."

"Pretty much," Chance acknowledged.

"Knew you would. Too much like me."

Chance nodded shortly. "Maybe."

Grant dropped one arm around his wife's shoulders. "Emma's the party-giver around here. Loves the hustle and bustle. She just tells me when to show up."

Emma gave his broad chest a playful slap, before looking at Chance. "It's true, you know. He'd much rather be out taking over small companies or sailing, or...well, just about anything."

Jennifer watched as a small smile curved Chance's lips, and to her surprise, a curl of something delightful spiraled through her in response. Oh, that probably wasn't a good sign.

"Then maybe we are more alike than I'd thought," Chance allowed as Grant took his outstretched hand and gave it a firm shake.

His father smiled. "I'll settle for a maybe. For now."

"Seems fair," Chance told him.

"All right, then," Emma spoke up. "Jennifer, I hope you're feeling better tomorrow. Why don't you take the day off?"

"Oh, that won't be—"

"A day off's not going to bring the world to an end," her employer told her firmly. Then she shifted a look at Chance. "You drive carefully.

Without Jennifer, I'd never get a thing done around here."

"Yes, ma'am," Chance said, and in seconds he had Jennifer turned around and headed for the front door. They skirted the edges of the party and avoided being stopped again. Their steps clicked on the cold marble of the main staircase, then echoed as they moved into the grand entry hall on the main floor. Here, the marble gleamed and shone in the spill of late-afternoon sunshine slashing through the wide front windows. Chance left her just long enough to grab their coats, and once she was bundled up, he ushered her outside into the bite of the cold Chicago wind.

"I'm parked just up the street," he said. "Why don't you wait here and I'll go get the car?"

"Thanks, I'd rather walk."

"Suit yourself," he said smiling, then offered her his arm.

Arms linked, they took the short flight of steps to the sidewalk below, crossed the narrow strip of lawn and turned onto Michigan Avenue.

"I can't believe you found a place to park around here."

He grinned at her and Jennifer sucked in a breath. That really was a devastating weapon he had tucked away. Thankfully, her defenses had been strengthened over the last two years.

"I'm a SEAL, remember? We excel at the impossible."

"I'll keep that in mind."

While they walked, he talked, as if somehow sensing that she wasn't in the mood to discuss her problems anymore tonight. She listened to stories of his and Doug's childhood, heard the pride in his voice when he talked about his mother and what she'd managed to accomplish all on her own. She hoped that one day Sarah would be as kind when talking about her.

God knows, she tried to be both mom and dad. But it wasn't easy. Despite having a great job with the most understanding employer in the free world, Jennifer was pushed every day, wondering how to get everything done. She had no idea at all how women with less going for them managed to survive.

"It must have been so hard for her," she finally said, looking up at him. The wind blew strands of blond hair across her face and she plucked them out of her way so she could see him clearly.

He stared off into the distance as if looking into years past and nodded. "Yeah, it was," he said, "but we didn't know that at the time. She made it look so easy. Mom wasn't the kind to sit around and whine about finding herself. Or wishing that things were different. She used to say that the only thing you could change in life was yourself. So do the best you can.''

''Smart woman.''

''Oh, yeah.'' He turned his head to look down at her and gave her yet another of those great smiles. ''She would have liked you.''

''Really? Why's that?''

''Because your daughter's so important to you.''

Something clutched at her heart, but Jennifer only said, ''She's everything to me.''

''I can see that.''

''That easy to read, huh?''

''Does the phrase *an open book* mean anything to you?''

Jennifer laughed in spite of herself. She'd never had much of a poker face. ''Mike used to say the reason I was so honest was because I just couldn't pull off a lie.''

''Good a reason as any,'' he said and stopped alongside a cherry-red SUV.

''This is yours?'' she asked and wondered why she was even surprised. If this wasn't a guy's car, she'd eat it.

''Rental,'' he said and opened her door. Holding it for her as she got in, he added, ''I'm just in town for a while.''

She automatically reached for the shoulder harness. ''Where do you go when you leave here?''

''Back to my SEAL team.''

"And then?"

"Won't know until just before I go."

He slammed the door, walked around the front of the car, then opened the driver's-side door. Sliding onto the front seat, he latched his seat belt, stuck the key in the ignition and turned it. The engine leapt into life with a muffled rumble of sound.

Shifting slightly in his seat, he winced and Jennifer asked, "Are you okay?"

"Yeah," he said. "I just keep forgetting to move slow. Think I pulled a few stitches is all."

Stitches? The question must have been written on her face, because he gave her a shrug and an it's-no-big-deal look before saying, "Took a hit on my last mission."

"A *hit?*" she asked, her gaze dropping to his side as if she could see right through his uniform. "You mean you were shot?"

"It's nothing major," he said. "Just cut through the meat."

"Ah," she muttered, with a sage nod. "A *minor* gunshot wound. And did you actually call it a flesh wound at the time, in the finest John Wayne tradition?"

His brows drew together as he watched her. "What's the problem here?"

"Oh, not a thing," she said and gripped her hands together in her lap as she turned her head to stare out the windshield. Just like Mike, she thought. They were cut from the same cloth. Dangerous jobs. Dismissive of hazards. No big deal. How could any sane person think it was no big deal to face the possibility of death as a matter of course? What was it that drove men—and some women—to take jobs that threatened their lives?

"Jennifer," he said, over the low roar of the engine, "you want to tell me what's got you so tense all of a sudden?"

She swiveled her head to look at him. The planes and hollows of his face stood out in stark relief. He looked hard and dangerous—but for the gentleness she could still read in his eyes.

"I don't get it," she finally blurted. "What is it about you guys?"

"Us guys?" he repeated, a half smile on his face. "Care to be more specific?"

"Men like you. And Mike."

"Your husband."

"My *late* husband," she corrected, then muttered, "I don't know why that phrase is used. It's not like he's going to be on time somewhere. He isn't late, for heaven's sake. He's dead."

"Jennifer—"

"No, I want to know," she said, meeting his gaze and holding it. "What is it that makes you deliberately seek out the kind of profession that endangers your lives? Is it for the thrills? The rush of constant peril?"

His mouth tightened briefly. "I've spent years in training to do my job, and I'm guessing your husband did, too. You don't put in that kind of effort just for the thrill of it."

"Then why?" she asked, knowing he was right. Mike had worked hard at being a police officer. He'd loved it. Had lived, breathed and eventually *died* for it. She couldn't ask him why now, so she wanted an answer from this man who lived his life the same way.

"To serve," he said softly, simply. "To help. To fight for my country. Sounds corny, huh? But that's the plain truth of it."

His words seemed to echo in the enclosed space as he went on.

"Military or cop, we do what has to be done. It's not for some rush," he said and added, "and I think you know that. It's not an easy life, but it's the only one I know. Or want. And I'm guessing it was the same for your husband."

Jennifer drew one long, shuddering breath and released it. Watching him, listening to him, she knew he was right. Felt it. And a part of her even agreed with him. But admitting that brave men were necessary and actually living with one were two different things. She'd put in her time in the trenches. She'd worried every time Mike left the house. And it hadn't kept him alive.

She wasn't interested in living with that kind of fear again.

No. There was only one person in her life now. Her daughter. And thoughts of Sarah were all she had time for. Anything else would just be a distraction right now. A distraction she didn't need.

Even if it was six feet two inches of solidly packed muscle encased in a snow-white naval uniform.

Four

"Turn right here," she said and watched the familiar neighborhood pass as Chance steered the SUV down her street. Oak Park, Illinois, came by its name honestly, she thought, not for the first time.

Ancient oaks lined nearly every street, stretching long, leafy arms across the avenues to form what in summer, were cool green tunnels that blunted the steamy heat. Now the first of the new leaves were just beginning to sprout, and the skeletal trees rattled their limbs together in the wind as if clamoring for their new spring outfits.

Jennifer smiled to herself as she noted the sidewalks that rolled up and down like cement waves.

Unlike other big cities, where the slightest bump in a sidewalk meant death to the offending tree, here city workers just slapped fresh cement atop the protruding roots. They protected their trees and the city was the better for it.

"It's a nice street," Chance said and she gave him a quick glance.

"Yes, it is," she agreed, and inwardly cringed. Well, one sure way to discourage him was to bore him to tears. But in her own defense, with thoughts of Sarah constantly simmering in her mind, it was hard to try to make conversation.

So instead of even trying, she looked at the houses as they passed. Some were like hers, old, with wide front porches supported by stone pillars. Others were brand-new, boasting lots of glass and sharp angles. Not too long ago the neighborhood had been dying, but in recent years young professionals had discovered the beauty of Oak Park and had infused it with new life. It was practically trendy now, and if Mike hadn't inherited their house from his late aunt, they never would have been able to afford to live there. "Frank Lloyd Wright's house is just around the corner."

"The architect?"

"Uh-huh," she said. "It's a lovely place even if it is a little on the modern side for me."

He slanted her a long glance. "Just an old-fashioned girl, are you?"

She shifted in her seat and folded her hands in her lap. "About some things, I guess," she admitted. "Like these old bungalow-type homes. They're just cozier…warmer somehow. They've got character."

"I think I know what you mean," he said, and she turned to look at him. He gave her a half smile. "The older places have weathered the storms. They've earned the right to be here."

An interesting way to put it, she thought. But so true. "I guess that's it," she said. "Some of these places have been here more than fifty years. Sheltering families, withstanding tornadoes—and all they need is a little care. A part of me even feels sorry for the poor houses that are torn down to make way for some spanking new glass-and-chrome disaster."

He laughed then. "A romantic. Who would have thought it?"

Romantic? Nope. Not her. Maybe once, she thought, remembering how young and naive she'd been when she'd married Mike. She'd looked at the world through rose-colored glasses. When they'd moved into his late aunt's cozy bungalow on this street, she'd assumed that they'd still be sitting on the front porch together when they were eighty.

But that plan had been buried with Mike, and now she considered herself more of a realist than a romantic. No more believing in happily ever after for *this* girl. Her fairy tale had ended. But there was no point in explaining all of that to Chance Barnett. He wouldn't be around long enough to care. He'd made no secret of the fact that he was itching to be gone. A couple more weeks and he'd be off living his dangerous life—which was just as well, she thought. Because she—she would still be here, trying to walk a minefield while carrying precious cargo.

And just the thought of Sarah was enough to bring her right back to the terrifying reality that was now her life.

"The house on the left is mine," she said abruptly, lifting one hand to point. "The blue one, with the wagon in front of the steps."

Her heart seized briefly as she realized that there was a very real chance that Sarah and her wagons and toys—the same ones Jennifer complained about being left all over—might not be a part of her life much longer. But no. She wouldn't even entertain the possibility. Hadn't the doctor told her this was a relatively simple operation? Hadn't he assured her that though there were always risks involved in surgery, this one was practically a cookie-cutter job?

Cookie-cutter.

How could anything requiring her daughter's tiny chest to be opened be considered cookie-cutter?

Tears leapt into her eyes and she blinked them back as Chance pulled into the driveway. Parked

directly in front of them was her own car, still list-
ing to one side on its flat rear tire. She'd come
outside that morning to find it like that, which ex-
plained why she'd been at the Connelly mansion
with no ride home.

And why she was now sitting here beside a man
whose very presence was a distraction she so didn't
need at the moment.

He put the car into Park and turned off the motor.
Instantly, a rush of silence filled the car and the
only sounds came from a group of kids two doors
down playing basketball against a garage. The
steady thump of the bouncing ball felt almost like
a heartbeat, and the minute that thought raced into
her brain, Jennifer pushed it out again.

"Looks like your car had an adventure," he said
quietly.

At his words, she smiled in spite of herself.
"When I was little, I used to think that when their
owners were asleep, cars would take off on their
own. You know, go for drives along the beach,
meet up with other cars at the garage to share a
quart of oil."

He chuckled.

"Apparently," she said on a sigh, "*my* car took
a bad bump somewhere along the road."

"So why didn't you fix it?"

"Gee," she said, giving her forehead a light slap,
"why didn't I think of that?"

"Dumb question, huh?"

"No," she said, "not really." After all, since Mike's death, she'd had to take care of lots of things on her own. Like stopped-up sinks or blown fuses. "I should be able to do it, but I just haven't taken my tire-changing class yet."

"How about I do it for you?"

She flicked him a quick glance. A part of her longed to say, That'd be great. But the smarter side of her knew that she didn't need to be indebted any further to Chance Barnett Connelly. Actually, the more distance she kept between herself and a man who could start her blood simmering with a look, the better. "No, that's okay. Thanks, but you really don't have to."

"I know I don't have to," he said, snatching the keys from the ignition and palming them. "But it's no big deal."

"Right," she said, grabbing for the door latch, "and black grease would look great on those dress whites of yours."

A moment ticked by before he gave her a wide, sheepish grin.

Something inside her turned over with a loud thud and slapped hard against her heart. Good grief.

He shrugged and said, "Oh, yeah. Forgot about that. Guess I'm really not in my best mechanic's outfit."

No, she thought, but his heartbreaker outfit looked just fine. Too fine.

And on that thought, she spoke up. "Well," she said, unhooking her shoulder strap and reaching for her purse on the floor, "thanks for the ride."

He opened his car door and got out, then walked around to her side of the car. She watched him come with an inward sigh. Apparently he wasn't going to just drop her off and race away. And she wasn't entirely sure how she felt about that.

He wasn't good for her equilibrium. Oh, he seemed nice enough, but for heaven's sake, she hardly knew him. Yet in the last few hours she'd wept all over his uniform—and Jennifer *never* cried—plus, she'd felt…*stirrings* deep within her and darn it, she wasn't interested in stirring anything but a pot of soup.

So, it was time to tell the navy man to go for a long sail to…somewhere. All she wanted now was to get inside, alone, check on Sarah and make a cup of tea.

Chance opened her door for her and extended one hand to help her down. Jennifer looked at his open palm for a long minute, trying to decide if she should take it or struggle out of the oversize car on her own. Instantly, an image of herself, skirt riding high on her thighs as she slid inelegantly from the too-high car, shot through her mind and just like that, her decision was made.

"Thanks," she said and slipped her hand into his. Warmth skittered up the length of her arm and splintered inside her chest, sending shafts of heat dancing throughout her body. His fingers curled around hers and she felt his grip right down to her bones.

"My pleasure," he murmured, his gaze meeting and holding hers.

Uh-oh.

The minute her feet hit the driveway, she pulled her hand free, but it didn't help. She felt his touch anyway, as surely as if he was still holding on to her. Curling her fingers into her palm, she deliberately ignored the sensation and gave him her best, brightest, phoniest smile.

"Well," she said, then paused to swallow hard and lower her voice just a notch or two, "I guess I'd better go inside now."

"I'll walk you to your door."

"That's not necessary," she began but saw the determination in his eyes, and knew that she wouldn't be getting rid of him that easily. Nodding, she headed for the front door, listening to the sounds of his footsteps right behind her. And she couldn't help wondering if the *S* in SEAL stood for Stubborn.

Or maybe Sexy.

Oh, good grief.

She pulled the screen door open and walked quickly across the wide front porch.

Chance watched her. Hell, he couldn't *stop* watching her. The sway of her hips, the brush of her hair against the collar of her dress, the trim line of calf and ankle. And then there was the vulnerable shine in her green eyes. Damn, the woman was enough to bring the strongest man to his knees.

And he wasn't exactly in peak condition at the moment.

When she stopped at the closed front door, he took just a moment to look around the cozy little screened-in porch. Rag rugs dotted the cement floor that had been painted a glossy barn-red. Dolls had been plunked down at a tiny table set for an imaginary tea party, and he felt a tug of tenderness for the sick little girl he'd yet to meet.

Chance shifted his gaze back to the woman in front of him and admiration for her crowded inside him. He knew exactly how hard her life was. His own mother had worked herself to an early death taking care of him and Douglas. He remembered how tight money had always been and how tired his mother usually was. But he also recalled clearly what it felt like to be loved unconditionally.

Recalling the look in Jennifer's green eyes when she'd told him about her daughter's problems, Chance knew that whatever Sarah's medical situation was, she at least could count on her mother's love.

But on the heels of that thought came other memories. Memories of the men his mother had dated and the way Chance had felt about them as they filed through their lives with numbing regularity. He couldn't blame his mother for wanting to find love. But he did blame those men for pretending to care about him and Doug and then disappearing without a backward glance when the relationship ended.

He'd long ago made a vow to steer clear of single mothers himself. He wasn't going to be one of those guys who blasted through a kid's life leaving behind nothing but a memory and a string of broken promises. And until today he'd kept that vow.

So what in the hell was he doing here?

Jennifer opened the door and stepped inside. Before he could ask himself too many more uncomfortable questions, Chance followed.

The first thing he noticed were the toys. Dolls and coloring books and stuffed animals littered the floor. The front door opened directly into the living room and from where he stood, he could see everything. Well-worn, overstuffed furniture crowded the small space and somehow managed to look inviting, rather than cramped. Doilies graced the tops of the highly-polished tables and a small, tidy fire burned in the hearth across the room. The walls were a soft peach color and dotted with framed family pictures. A doorway off to the right led into what looked like the kitchen and to the left was a darkened hallway that probably branched off into the bedrooms.

"Mrs. Sorenson?" Jennifer called out as she walked into the living room and tossed her purse onto the closest table. "I'm home."

"In here." An older, female voice answered and Jennifer headed straight for it, moving toward the hallway on the left. She seemed to have forgotten all about Chance and he knew damn well he should leave. But he didn't. Instead, he walked along behind her, despite knowing that he had no business pushing into her life any further than he had already.

Somehow, for some reason, he just wasn't ready to leave yet. And he didn't really want to think about why.

Four doorways opened off the short hall, but Jennifer made right for the last one on the right. Looking over her head, Chance could see the pale-yellow paint on the wall and what looked like a mural of daisies. Then he was in the doorway, and there he stopped while Jennifer headed straight for the crib on the far wall.

"How is she?" she asked.

A short, round woman with gray-streaked red hair and deeply-etched laugh lines gave her a smile.

"She's fine now. Wanted to play, then tuckered herself out, poor sweetie."

Jennifer reached into the crib and smoothed one hand across her daughter's dirty forehead.

"Should have cleaned her up, I know," Mrs. Sorenson was saying, "but she was just so tired, I thought, why bother?"

"It's fine," Jennifer said. "I'll clean her up later."

"Well," the woman said, picking up her paperback book from the table beside the rocking chair she'd been occupying up until a moment ago, "if you need anything, you give a shout. Although," she added thoughtfully, "it looks as though you have all the help you'll need for a while."

Jennifer glanced at her and saw the speculative gleam in her neighbor's eyes as the woman gave Chance a slow once-over. Inwardly she sighed, knowing that sooner or later, her babysitter was going to want details about the tall, gorgeous hunk of sailor standing on the threshold. But not now.

"Eva Sorenson," Jennifer said, "Commander Chance Barnett Connelly."

The older woman gave him a quick grin. "I love a man with three names."

His grin matched hers. "Then I'll keep all three of them, for sure."

"Hmm," Eva mused, "cute and quick, too." She tossed a sidelong look at Jennifer. "Watch out for this one, honey. He's probably got a half dozen girls in every port.''

''Only half a dozen?'' Chance asked, his voice teasing.

''Quality, not quantity,'' Eva retorted.

''I'll remember that.''

Briefly, she inclined her head toward Jennifer, then warned not too subtly, ''See that you do.'' Then she inhaled sharply and said to no one in particular, ''Jim'll be wanting his dinner soon, so I'd better go. You know how that man is when he isn't fed on time.''

''Cheerful?'' Jennifer asked, since she couldn't ever remember seeing anything but a smile on Jim Sorenson's broad features.

Chuckling, Eva said, ''Hey, living with a perpetual optimist isn't all a picnic, you know.''

And then she was gone, slipping out the door and leaving Chance and Jennifer alone with the sleeping child. If he had any sense at all, Chance told himself, he'd be hot on the babysitter's heels, headed for his car and then his hotel.

But apparently his brain was on vacation, because he walked farther into the room and didn't stop until he was standing beside Jennifer staring down at the little girl lying beneath a flowered quilt.

He threw a quick glance at the woman beside him and noted the worry staining her eyes despite the soft smile curving her lips. She looked up at him briefly and said, "Chance, meet Sarah."

Love filled her voice and Chance couldn't help being moved by it. Then he shifted his gaze to the child with the dirty face and lopsided pigtails that weren't much bigger than the barrettes holding them in place. Her tiny, rosebud mouth was parted in sleep and as he watched, she lifted one grubby little fist and rubbed her eyes before rolling onto her side. Then she blindly groped around for a battered stuffed bear that was lying just out of her reach.

Chance moved the scruffy beast with one missing ear in closer and the little girl grabbed for it, latching on to his hand instead. Her tiny fingers clutched at him and held on tight.

A long deep breath rushed from his lungs.

And just like that, he fell in love.

Five

As that thought shot through his brain, Chance jerked back as if he'd been hit by a stray bullet. Absently, he watched the tiny girl's now-empty hand reach for and grab her stuffed animal. She pulled it close, buried her nose in its ratty fur and sighed in satisfaction.

Chance shoved his hands into his pockets and tried not to notice that he could still feel the toddler's surprisingly strong grip around his fingers.

"Are you okay?" Jennifer whispered, and he threw her a quick, wary glance.

"Yeah," he said, moving another uneasy step back from the crib. "Yeah, I'm fine."

Good job, Barnett, he told himself. Hell, he'd been in dozens of tight situations. Stared down the barrels of way too many guns. Slipped into and out of hostile nations without turning a hair.

And one soft stirring for a sick little girl had him ready to bolt for cover. He pulled one hand free of his pocket and scrubbed it across his face. This he hadn't counted on.

A pretty woman. A jolt of desire. Okay. But he hadn't planned on tenderness and wasn't at all sure what to do about it now that it had entered the picture.

"You don't look okay," Jennifer said and led the way quietly from the room.

Not surprising. A man suddenly slapped with feelings he'd never encountered before was liable to look as though he'd been hit in the head with a two-by-four. It was just that the girl was so tiny. So helpless. And damn it, a kid that small just shouldn't have to be sick. Scowling, he pushed those thoughts aside and concentrated on the woman in front of him.

He was only a step or two behind her and even with his thoughts churning, he managed to lower his gaze long enough to admire the sway of her hips and the shapeliness of her calves. Damn, but high heels did amazing things for a woman's legs.

And as dangerous as it was to be thinking about

Jennifer's legs, it was safer than dwelling on other, even more dangerous thoughts.

As soon as she walked into the living room, she stepped out of those heels and instantly became softer, more vulnerable somehow. And just as quickly, Chance's internal radar sent out a warning ping. Admiration for a single mother was all well and good. But did he really want another complication in his life? Wasn't dealing with a newly-inherited family enough at the moment?

"Hello?" she asked, prodding gently. "I asked if you were okay, remember?"

"I'm fine," he said firmly, silently congratulating himself on the fascinating conversation. Hell, what had happened to the glibness he was noted for with women? "Just tired, I guess. Not completely back up to speed yet."

Her features paled a bit, but she recovered quickly, he gave her that.

"How badly were you wounded?"

"Like you said before—just a flesh wound."

Jennifer folded her arms across her middle, dipped her head briefly then looked up at him again. "I'm sorry about that."

"Don't be."

"No, I shouldn't have said it."

"I'll live," he assured her and took a step closer. He couldn't seem to help himself. Everything about her drew him in. She touched something inside him and though he knew he should be fighting it, he surrendered to the feeling instead.

Her scent drifted to him. Her eyes looked wide, troubled, and for some damn reason, Chance wanted to do something—*anything*—to help. As he came closer, she shook her head in warning.

"Chance," she said, then corrected herself, "Commander Barnett—Connelly— Blast it."

A flicker of a smile danced across his face and was gone again, but in that instant, Jennifer knew she was in trouble. This man was pure, undiluted, top-grade sex appeal.

"Chance will do," he said and the amusement in his tone told her that he knew exactly what she was up to. Trying to put distance between them.

His amber eyes focused on her and it was like looking up into twin topazes. Her breath hitched and she wanted to back up, but there was simply nowhere to go. For the first time, she resented the fact that her living room was so darn tiny. A little maneuvering room was needed here and she was flat out of luck.

"Look, I appreciate you giving me a ride home, but—"

"But you'd rather I left now."

"Exactly," she said. "No offense, it's just—" Why couldn't she talk? Or think? He was too close, that was it. That broad chest. The startling white of his uniform against the deep tan of his skin. The cluster of medals and ribbons pinned above his heart.

Medals.

For bravery? For being shot?

For living the kind of dangerous life that had already robbed her of a husband?

Instantly, her heartbeat evened out, her breathing came just a bit easier and she felt control again. That's all she'd have to do. Remind herself continually of the fact that Chance Barnett Connelly was a man to whom life equaled danger.

And she'd had enough danger in her life already, thanks very much.

She lifted both hands, palms out, to stop his ever-increasing advance. It worked.

"What?" he asked, and he was so close, she felt the brush of his breath dust across her forehead.

A whisper of goose bumps raced along her spine, but Jennifer ignored them. She *had* to.

"This isn't a good idea at all," she said, "and I think you know it, too."

"Maybe," he said and his gaze moved over her features as surely as a caress.

She shivered, but shook her head. Steeling herself, she said, "I'm not interested in joining your group of 'girls in every port.'"

He actually looked offended. "Hey, I didn't say that. Your baby-sitter did."

"Yeah, but she was right," Jennifer muttered,

knowing it had to be true. No unmarried man who looked like Chance was hurting for company.

He took a half step back and she breathed a little easier.

"No, she wasn't," he said.

Jennifer looked up into his eyes and caught a glint of anger shining in those golden depths. Well, better anger than the desire that had been there a moment before. Much easier to deal with.

"It really doesn't matter, does it?"

"Yeah, it does," he said, his gaze locking onto hers. "There's something between us, Jennifer. Call it chemistry. Hell, call it lust."

"I'd rather not call it anything," she said.

"Ignoring it won't make it go away."

"Worth a shot," she quipped nervously and a moment later cringed to realize that by saying that, she'd actually admitted that there was something to ignore.

He nodded slowly and moved away. "I'm gonna go now."

Thank heaven.

"But I'll be back."

And as he walked toward the front door, Jennifer couldn't help wondering if that last statement had been a warning or a promise.

It turned out to be both.

The clatter of two small feet on the linoleum announced Sarah just a moment before that little voice shouted, "Chanz here!"

Expectation, excitement and dread all coiled together to form a knot in her throat that Jennifer dutifully swallowed back. Wrist-deep in soapy water, she looked back over her shoulder and smiled at her daughter.

"Tell Chance mommy's coming, all right?"

"'kay," the child said and spun around to run back the way she'd come.

"*Walk,* Sarah," Jennifer called out and was pleased to see the girl instantly slow down. Now shuffling her feet in obvious disgust, she left the room.

Chanz. Her daughter was nuts about Chance Barnett, and the feeling appeared to be mutual. He'd spent so much time here in the last three days that Jennifer now automatically set an extra plate on the table for him. Somehow, he'd managed to invade her life, captivate her daughter and send her own hormones on a white-water raft ride—all with very little effort.

Shaking soapsuds off her fingers, Jennifer grabbed a dish towel, dried her hands, then reached up to smooth her hair. Silly. She didn't *want* to look good for Chance Barnett, so what did she care if her hair was a mess?

Just a female reaction, that was all. It didn't mean anything. It didn't mean—

"Well, hi there, Chuckles!"

Chance's voice floated through the living room and into the kitchen where it raced up the length of Jennifer's spine and tickled the base of her neck. She hardly heard Sarah's delighted laughter over the roaring in her own ears. Her stomach took a nosedive and her breath came fast and hard.

For heaven's sake, she was acting like some teenager waiting for her prom date to pick her up. This wasn't a date, she reminded herself. And she sure as heck wasn't a teenager. So why couldn't she stop these ridiculous flutters of excitement that rippled through her whenever he was close?

Shaking her head, she muttered, "Quit stalling and get out there. Otherwise he'll think you're hiding from him."

She was, of course, but he didn't have to know that.

Chance sat on the couch, Sarah on his lap. The little girl held a book open and was stabbing at the pictures with one index finger.

"Tuttle."

"Turtle," he corrected gently and smoothed one hand over the back of the child's head.

"Yes," Sarah agreed, nodding sharply. "Tuttle."

Chance grinned and, as if sensing her presence, looked up directly into Jennifer's gaze. She felt the power of that stare right down to the soles of her feet. The man really packed a wallop.

"We're reading," he said.

"So I see." And darned if they didn't look like father and daughter. So cozy. So comfortable with each other. So— Don't go there, she warned herself even as she started walking toward the twosome.

"Momma come sit, too," Sarah announced, then shifted her gaze back to the book. "Doggie."

"Sure is," Chance agreed.

The little girl reached for his cheek and turned his face to hers. "Me wanna doggie."

"We talked about this, baby," Jennifer said, drawing Sarah off Chance's lap to sit with her. "You can have a doggie when you're all better."

"Me better," the girl insisted.

"Not yet," Jennifer said, past the aching knot in her throat, "but soon."

"Now. Better now."

She wished that were true, but looking into her little girl's face, Jennifer could see the dark violet shadows beneath her big brown eyes. Her skin was as pale as fine porcelain and just as fragile. Her little body might look sturdy, but it held a damaged heart, and until that was fixed, Jennifer would take no chances with her baby.

Her family.

"Wanna doggie," Sarah pleaded, leaning in and

tipping her head to one side for that extra special emphasis all children seemed to know instinctively.

"I'm sorry, honey, the answer is no."

Her bottom lip shot out and she folded her chubby arms across her chest. Then with as much dignity as an eighteen-month-old could manage, she stomped out of the room.

"No dog?"

Jennifer slanted the man beside her a look. "Not until she's well enough to play with one."

"It might help her to—"

"I know you mean well," Jennifer said, interrupting him before he could side with Sarah against her, "but she's my daughter and I have to do what I think is best for her."

"I'm not arguing," he said, lifting both hands in mock surrender.

"You were going to."

He looked like he might argue that, then gave it up and admitted sheepishly, "Yeah, I was."

"It's not easy saying no to her," Jennifer said on a sigh as she slumped back against the cushions.

"I noticed," he said with a chuckle. "I think she had my number from day one. All she has to do is look up at me with those big brown eyes and I'm her sucker."

Yes, Jennifer had seen that. He'd developed a special relationship with Sarah, and, though it worried her a little, she was also pleased. Sarah didn't have enough family in her life, and no close male relatives. It was good, wasn't it, to have Chance here, even for a little while? Or was she making a mistake in letting the two become friends? After all, when Chance left, as he would eventually, Sarah would miss him desperately.

And not, she thought with an inward twinge, just Sarah.

A crash from the other room shattered that train of thought.

''Sarah?''

Jennifer shot up from the love seat and raced across the room, her heart pounding in time with her hurried steps. ''Sarah honey?'' she called, ''Are you all right?''

Dashing through the hallway, she rounded the corner and came to a sudden stop. Sarah stood in the center of the room, staring at the toppled doll-house, lying on its side on the floor. She must have collided with the little table it sat on when she ran into the room. But it didn't matter. All that mattered was that she was safe. Relief coursed through Jennifer's body with the strength and overwhelming power of a river bursting its banks.

Huge tears formed in the little girl's eyes as she looked up at her mother. Jennifer dropped to her knees, gathered the girl up close and held her tightly. ''Are you all right, baby? Are you hurt? You have to be careful, sweetheart. You shouldn't run. Just walk, all right? It's okay, don't cry. Don't cry..."

Her soothing words flowed into a steady stream of comforting sounds and hums, and Chance stood in the doorway, watching. Morning sunlight poured through the gleaming windowpanes to fall like a golden spotlight on Jennifer and her child as the two of them clung together like the only survivors of a tragedy.

He felt distanced from them, left out of this tender moment, and it surprised him to note just how much that bothered him. Inhaling deeply, he leaned one shoulder against the doorjamb and kept his gaze locked on the two females who had somehow become too important to him. His own heart rate was just slowing down. Amazing how the sound of a crash could scare you when a kid was involved. Hell, he'd come through firefights with less of a reaction. Yet as the seconds ticked past into minutes and still Jennifer hadn't released the girl, he began to wonder.

He wondered if Jennifer had always been this protective of the child, or if it was as a direct result of the heart problem that she was so terrified.

Six

"**W**hat is he up to?" Jennifer stared across Emma's office at the soft, soothing Monet hanging on the wall opposite her. But neither the violin music drifting out of the stereo nor the filmy greens and blues of Monet's gardens were going to be enough to calm the nerves jangling throughout her body.

"Why does he have to be 'up to' anything?" Emma answered the question with one of her own.

Sliding a glance at her employer, Jennifer gave her a rueful smile and said, "You would have made a good psychiatrist. Get the patient to answer her own questions."

"Oh, honey," Emma said, leaning forward to place her hand atop Jennifer's, "you're not a patient and you sure as heck don't need a shrink."

"I'm not so sure," Jennifer muttered with a shake of her head. Then she took hold of Emma's hand and gave it a hard squeeze before releasing it to lean back in her chair. "Lately I feel like I'm losing my mind."

"Of course you do," the older woman said. "You're worried sick over your baby."

True, Jennifer thought, as Sarah's sweet little face appeared in her mind. Every waking moment and most of her dreams were filled with half-frenzied, panic-filled thoughts of a nebulous, dangerous future. But to be honest, if only with herself, Chance was taking up a lot of time in her thoughts, too.

Blast it.

Heck, blast *him.*

She hadn't asked for this. Hadn't wanted any more complications in her life than already existed. She didn't need this right now. He was a distraction. Oh, a gorgeous one, granted, but still a distraction.

And she couldn't afford to have her concentration scattered right now. It didn't have anything to do with him personally, of course. It was just a bad time for her to try to have a relationship.

Jennifer groaned inwardly. Heck, even *she* didn't believe that.

There wasn't another man alive who could distract her from her worries right now. It was only Chance. Him. That smile. Those eyes. The way his voice rippled across her skin and made her think of hot summer nights. The gentleness he always showed Sarah.

"Oh, for pity's sake," she muttered and clapped one hand over her eyes.

Emma chuckled softly and took a seat beside her on the small floral damask sofa. "He's getting to you, isn't he?"

Jennifer parted her fingers wide enough to be able to peer at her employer. "Do I have to answer that?"

"Ah, honey," the woman crowed, "you just did!"

Emma Connelly was more than Jennifer's boss, she was a friend—and the closest thing to a mother Jennifer had. Which was why the woman felt completely at ease offering her opinions, whether they were asked for or not. But to be fair, it wasn't nosiness prompting her. It was concern. Emma'd been nothing but kindness itself ever since Jennifer had started working for her. And Jennifer thanked heaven every day that she had a good job with excellent insurance benefits.

But that didn't mean she was going to bare her

soul and start confessing the legion of confusing feelings she had for Emma's stepson.

Apparently, though, she didn't have to.

"Face it, child," the woman was saying with a grin, "you never stood a chance. That man's got his daddy's charm, and add that to how good he looks in his uniform, and, well—" Emma shrugged good-naturedly. "He just plain outgunned you."

"Maybe," Jennifer admitted as a mental image of Chance filled her mind and caused her heartbeat to stagger drunkenly. It took every ounce of her will to combat that feeling, but she managed. "But, Emma, I just can't deal with him now. There's Sarah to worry about and—"

"Darlin'," Emma interrupted, "I won't tell you not to worry, you'll do that anyway. Any mother would. But we've got the best doctor there is to perform the operation. Her hospital bills are taken care of."

Jennifer opened her mouth, but Emma cut her off.

"And no arguments, either. I don't want you worried about meeting deductibles or filling out paperwork." She sat up straight, picked up Jennifer's hand and patted it gently. "As for Chance, I'm not saying you should throw caution to the wind here. But on the other hand, where's the harm in enjoying the company of a handsome man? Where's the harm in having a bit of something for yourself in the middle of a trying time?''

"Emma..." She didn't mean any harm, Jennifer knew. But Emma didn't understand that even if Jennifer was interested in a man right now, it wouldn't be Chance. All fire and danger, he wasn't exactly the home-and-hearth type. "Don't go building fantasies, okay? He's only here temporarily and—''

"Honey, I'm not booking the church," Emma said softly. "All I'm saying is that you should try to relax a little. If Chance wants to offer you a strong shoulder to lean on during a hard time, why not take him up on it?''

Jennifer shook her head and smiled. "You know, women's libbers around the country would howl if they could hear you.''

"Twaddle," Emma blurted with a wave of one hand, effectively dismissing hordes of irate feminists. "There's a difference between being a strong woman and a hard one.'' Standing up, she ran the flat of her hands down the front of her meadow-green Chanel suit while she continued. "Men and women weren't meant to stand alone, sugar. We complement each other's strengths and weaknesses. That's the whole point.''

"Sure, in a perfect world," Jennifer said on a sigh.

"Nothing's perfect, Jennifer," Emma said, "but

it doesn't have to be as complicated as you make it, either.''

"Maybe," Jennifer conceded, more to end the conversation than for any other reason. She knew Emma meant well, but she also knew that her employer, despite her logical mind and keen business sense, was a romantic at heart. And there was nothing Emma would like better than for Chance and Jennifer to strike enough sparks off each other to ignite an eternal flame.

But that wasn't possible. First off, there was no such thing as eternal. No happily ever afters outside of fairy tales. The world just didn't work that way. Yet Jennifer was pretty sure she'd never be able to convince Emma of that. So what was the point of trying?

"Now," the other woman was saying, "it's late. Why don't you go on home to that baby of yours?"

Automatically Jennifer checked her wristwatch and then, frowning, looked up and said, "It's only three, Emma. I work until five."

"You work until I say you're finished for the day," her employer corrected gently. "Now get yourself home."

A little stab of guilt flashed within her briefly as Jennifer thought of the mountains of letters she still had to get signed and mailed. But in the next instant, she decided that if her boss wasn't worried about them, why should she be? Besides, it'd be fun to get home early and spend some time with Sarah. Nothing strenuous, of course, she couldn't risk that. But they could sit on a blanket in the sun and watch the clouds.

Just thinking about it made her smile, so she stood up and walked to her desk before she could change her mind. "All right, I will."

"Good. And don't you come back until after that baby's well and home again."

Swinging her purse strap over her shoulder, Jennifer turned and stared at her boss. "I can't do that. The surgery's not for a few days and then—" She shook her head as if to clear the mental picture of her daughter's ordeal. "There's too much to do. The correspondence alone—"

"Poo."

"I beg your pardon?"

"Poo on the letters," Emma said sternly, walking across the room to stand directly in front of her. Cupping Jennifer's cheeks in her hands, she said, "I can take care of myself for a while. You spend time with your baby—*with* pay. And I'll take no arguments here, honey."

Jennifer had seen that steely look in Emma's eyes before and knew it signaled the fact that her mind was made up and already set in concrete. Slowly, she nodded. "All right, then," she said and was rewarded with a smile. "Just don't discover that you can get along without me, okay?"

"Not a chance, honey. Your job'll be here waiting for you."

"Thanks, Emma," she said. "Thanks for everything."

"You're welcome. Now get going."

Jennifer did as she was told and headed for the door. Before she could leave the room, though, Emma's voice stopped her briefly.

"Say hello to Chance for me."

Jennifer glanced back over her shoulder. "He's staying here at the mansion. You'll see him before I will." She hoped.

"Uh-huh," Emma said.

"You're hopeless."

"Hope*ful*, honey. There's a difference."

Shaking her head, Jennifer headed down the hall and toward the staircase. At least with the time off she'd been given, she wouldn't be running into Chance at the mansion anymore. And that would be for the best.

So why wasn't she happier about that?

He'd had no idea it would be this much fun.

Someone should have told him what it was like to spend time around kids.

But, Chance admitted silently, if they had, he wouldn't have believed them anyway. Besides, maybe all kids weren't as terrific as this one.

He looked down into Sarah's big brown eyes and

felt himself go all soft inside. Like her mother, she had the ability to touch something within him that he hadn't even been aware of.

In the last week or so he'd spent so much time with Jennifer and Sarah that he almost couldn't imagine living any other way. How had he gotten along without fierce hugs from tiny arms? How had he managed to get through his whole life without seeing Jennifer's lips curve in a smile? Without seeing her eyes light up with pleasure or the way her hair seemed to damn near sparkle in the sunlight?

"Cha-anz," Sarah wheedled, somehow managing to make his name two syllables. "Sving, Chanz," she said, grabbing a tiny fistful of his pant-leg and shaking it.

"Sving?" he repeated with a laugh. "What are you, Swedish?"

"Sving." Sarah's bottom lip jutted out and Chance laughed. Hard not to. But dutifully, he picked her up, set her onto the swing and locked her into the baby seat. Then moving behind her, he gave her a small push and listened to the musical sound of her laughter.

She was magic. Pure and simple. And some day this kid was going to have the boys lined up outside her door. But as soon as that thought hit, he realized that he wouldn't be around then. He wouldn't know about her first skinned knee, her first bike ride, her first crush, her first date. He wouldn't be there to threaten those hormone-charged teenaged boys. He wouldn't know if she was happy or sad or lonely or laughing.

Hell, she wouldn't even remember him.

And with his next breath, he wondered if Jennifer would remember him—or want to remember him. Strange, for so many years, he'd done his best to be forgettable. He'd never had a relationship that had lasted for more than a week or two. But that had been the plan. He hadn't wanted a woman waiting at home for him. Hadn't wanted to have to worry about anyone but himself.

Well, it had worked like a charm.

There was no one who gave a damn if he lived or died. Except for his brother, of course, and that was completely different. That fact had never bothered him before. But it did now.

Ever since he'd looked into a pair of eyes greener than the sea. Ever since he'd stood alongside a short, curvy woman whose scent was enough to open up every closed door inside him. His back teeth ground together and his mind filled with images of him and Jennifer locked in a full body embrace. Want coursed through him and he knew a desire he'd never known before. This woman had reached him as no one else ever had.

The way she moved, the way she talked, the way she loved her daughter—everything about her made him hunger for what he'd never wanted before. And he knew damn well she wasn't interested. Jennifer and Sarah were a unit. The two of them were a solid wall, shutting out everyone else—including him.

Something cold and empty opened up inside him and to avoid thinking about it, he slowed the swing, unhooked Sarah's belt and picked her up, cradling her against his chest. For one long moment, he enjoyed the sturdy weight of her in his arms and the feel of her soft cheek pressed to his. How was it possible to love so much, so quickly?

And how would he ever leave her and her mother?

Sunshine poured down from a clear April sky and spattered the backyard with dappled shade from the surrounding trees. It was a picture-perfect scene. All that was missing was Jennifer.

Easing back from the baby a bit, he looked her dead in the eye and asked, "So, you think Mommy's going to be mad about the swing set?"

"Mommy?" Sarah's smile widened.

"Yeah, she has that effect on me, too," he admitted. Then, walking around the edge of the newly-installed play gym, he held Sarah at the top of the slide, one arm wrapped firmly around her middle. "You ready?" he asked.

She nodded fiercely, sending her tiny pigtails fluttering in the soft breeze.

"No, don't!"

Startled at the unexpected voice, Chance tightened his hold on the baby and looked across the yard to the back door. Jennifer stood on the threshold and even from a distance, he read the anger in her eyes.

Well, hell. Not exactly the reaction he'd been hoping for.

"What are you doing?" she demanded as she marched across the patio and then the grass. She stopped alongside the slide, reached up and plucked Sarah from his grasp. Tucking her carefully against her body, Jennifer then did a quick check, making sure her daughter was all right.

Chance bit back his irritation. Did she really think he couldn't be trusted to take care of a child?

The baby, picking up on her mother's tension, instantly began to sniffle and cry. Jennifer soothed her with a rocking motion and a few pats on her back—all the while shooting daggers at Chance.

"You're home early," he said, hoping to defuse a situation he didn't entirely understand.

"Just in time, apparently."

"What's that supposed to mean?"

"Where's Mrs. Sorenson?" she asked, looking around the yard as if expecting the older woman to leap up from behind a shrub.

Chance shrugged. "I told her she could go home early and I'd watch the baby."

"*You* told her?" she repeated, swinging her gaze back to his.

"Well, yeah," Chance said, shoving his hands into his pockets and stalling a bit. This wasn't at all how he'd imagined her reaction. Hell, he'd worked his butt off, deciphering instructions that read like Greek and putting this playground together in a matter of hours. He'd expected a delighted coo of appreciation for his efforts and maybe even an enthusiastic kiss. Good thing he wasn't a man to disappoint easily. "I was here and there was no point in both of us watching one little girl, so…"

"You're unbelievable," she muttered, shaking her head and staring at him as though he had three eyes, all of them blind.

At the sound of her mother's upset tone, the baby started crying in earnest. Now she was beginning to hit notes only dogs would hear.

Chance winced in sympathy and tried to figure out where he'd gone wrong. Things had been fine a minute ago. But then, Pearl Harbor on December 6, 1941, had been a pretty quiet place, too.

Jennifer started in on him again and he figured the only sure way to keep from getting killed was to pay attention.

"Mrs. Sorenson is *my* baby-sitter. You don't tell her when to stay or leave."

"But I was here and—" Why was he defending himself? She was being totally unreasonable. Couldn't she see that? Hell, he'd spent all day putting together a child's fantasy of a swing set, complete with slide and sandbox. He glanced over his shoulder at the bright blue-and-green monstrosity and his earlier pride in his handiwork shot right down the tubes.

"Why?"

"Why what?"

"Why *any* of this?" she demanded. "Start with why are you here?"

He shoved one hand along the side of his head and just for a minute, wished that the military would allow longer hair. It would have given him something to grab hold of and yank.

"I had to put the swing set together, for one," he said and before he could elaborate, she cut him off.

"Speaking of that, who told you to buy that in the first place?" Her gaze quickly scraped over his prize before settling back on him again. "I can't afford a swing set."

Okay now. Enough was enough. He hadn't asked her for a dime and she damn well knew it. "I bought it. As a gift. For Sarah."

Jennifer's eyes flashed and he knew this was going to get worse before it got better. Damn it, what was the woman's problem, anyway? Couldn't a man do something nice without being thrown on the barbecue and roasted?

"What?" she asked, sarcasm dripping from the

words. "The store was all out of stuffed animals, so you had to buy a swing set?"

"Sving," Sarah cried, burying her head in the curve of her mother's neck.

"Hah!" Chance shouted in victory and pointed at the crying baby. "*She* likes it!"

"*She* likes ice cream for dinner," Jennifer pointed out. "That doesn't mean it's good for her!"

Sarah let out a wail that tore at Chance's heart.

"Wanna sving…"

"Not now, honey," Jennifer murmured. "You could get hurt. Besides, you have to rest."

"She won't get hurt," Chance said and couldn't quite hide the impatience in his voice.

Her gaze should have sizzled him on the spot. "You can guarantee that, I suppose?"

"No," he said, folding his arms across his chest in a defensive position he felt he needed. Actually, he wouldn't have minded a flak jacket, either. Still, he tried to be the voice of reason. Hell, somebody had to. "But, Jen, kids get hurt all the time. It's a normal part of childhood."

She drew her head back and glared at him through narrowed eyes. Twin spots of red stained her cheeks and her breath came so fast and furious, it was a wonder she didn't hyperventilate. "Sarah's not a normal kid, though, is she? She has a heart condition. She shouldn't be running around or swinging or sliding or whatever else thing you have set up here.''

''I wouldn't have let her get too tired,'' he said, offended that she would think he wouldn't be careful of the child.

''And are you a doctor? You know how much tired is good and how much is bad?''

''No, but—''

''She's *my* daughter, Chance,'' Jennifer said. ''I have to do what I think is best for her.''

''And that's what?'' he asked. ''Basically just sitting in her room?''

''If that's what it takes to keep her healthy, yes,'' Jennifer snapped.

''What kind of life is that?'' he asked, remembering how only minutes ago, Sarah had been laughing and enjoying herself, and wondering how it had all ended so abruptly. And why was he fighting with Jennifer when all he really wanted to do was grab her to him and take her mouth in a slow, deep kiss?

''A safe one,'' she said.

''Jennifer,'' he said gently, moving in closer, laying one hand on her shoulder, ''you have to let her be a kid, too.''

The anger in her eyes flickered out, like a match in a windstorm, and just as quickly a sheen of tears rose up and she blinked frantically, trying to keep them at bay.

"I want to," she said, shaking her head as she looked up at him. "But I can't. I have to keep her safe. She's all I have." Her arms came around her baby and held her tightly. "She's sick. She has to be careful. I have to be careful for her. She depends on me. And I don't know what I'd do if I lost her…"

An invisible fist grabbed Chance's heart and squeezed it, hard. Reaching out, he gathered Jennifer and the baby and drew them into the circle of his arms. Cradling the two females who'd so captured his heart, he stood in the dappled shade and silently made a vow to do everything he could to protect both of them.

"You won't lose her," he whispered as he rested his chin atop Jennifer's head.

She snuggled in closer to him, wrapping her free arm around his middle. "Is that a promise?"

"You're damn right it is," he said and held her tighter, as if the strength of his arms alone could keep the three of them safe from any dangers the world had to offer.

Seven

The next few days flew by in a blur of worry and fear. Jennifer tried to hide her concerns from Sarah, but the baby was just too perceptive. Picking up on her mother's tension, the little girl was whiny and pretty much miserable. If it hadn't been for Chance, the two of them would have driven each other nuts, she was sure.

But Chance *had* been there—nearly every minute. He arrived right after breakfast and wouldn't leave until well after dinner. Since Sarah's medical problems had been discovered, there were any number of people in Jennifer's life who insisted she call them if she needed anything. And undoubtedly, they meant it. But Chance was different. He didn't wait to be asked—he was just there, doing whatever he could to help, even if it was just listening to Jennifer talk, or reading a story to Sarah.

He'd become a part of their lives and she wasn't even sure how it had happened. The cold, logical, reasonable part of her brain kept screaming at her to use caution. To keep a safe distance between them. And she knew darn well she should be listening to such solid advice.

But on the other hand…she looked across the room at the man sitting on her sofa, holding her sleeping daughter, and her heart lurched in her chest. Not easy to stand firm against a man who not only sent sparks of awareness skittering through your bloodstream, but also managed to show such tenderness toward your child.

It had been too long, she told herself firmly, as Chance stood up and smiled at her.

"I think she's down for the count," he whispered, and walked closer to her.

She's not the only one, Jennifer thought, thankful that the one thing Commander Wonderful couldn't do was read minds. "I'll take her," she said and scooped her arms beneath Chance's as he eased the baby into her care. Skin brushed over skin, heat shimmered, breath quickened. Jennifer pulled in a gulp of air and told herself she was being an idiot. She wouldn't make more out of this than there was.

"She's gonna be a heartbreaker one day," he whispered, and she wished he would quit doing that. When his voice was just a hush of sound, the word *sexy* didn't even come close to describing it. Then he added, "Like her mother," and Jennifer felt that odd rushing sensation coursing through her veins. It was as if every ounce of her blood was racing south of the border to pool in one achy spot that throbbed with every beat of her heart.

She swallowed hard, told herself *again* to get a grip and said, "One day's a long way off. Right now I'm just concerned with getting her through the surgery tomorrow and getting her well."

"She will be," Chance said and reached out to skim a lock of her hair behind Jennifer's ear. His fingertips brushed her skin, then slid down the length of her neck before falling away, and Jennifer shivered slightly in response. Heck, she couldn't help it.

A woman would have to be *dead* to not respond to this man.

"I'll be back in a minute," she muttered and escaped into the hallway, carrying her precious bundle. She walked into Sarah's darkened room, giving a quick glance at the butterfly night-light on the wall. Soft, muted colors strained through the butterfly's wings to lay patches of red and yellow and blue across the floor.

Sarah pulled in a breath and Jennifer's heart

caught. She was just so tiny. So helpless. And she was counting on her mother for so much. To keep her safe. And well. And happy. Jennifer was doing her best. Now she could only hope it would be enough.

She laid the baby down in her bed and pulled the blanket up to cover her. Smoothing one hand over her silky, fine hair, Jennifer hummed a series of low-pitched notes that didn't add up to a song and lost herself for a moment in the wonder of watching her baby sleep.

Which probably helped to explain why she didn't hear Chance enter the room until he was standing right beside her at the crib.

"You move too quietly," she said in a barely heard whisper.

"The government pays me to be sneaky," he said just as softly.

She turned her head to look up at him and caught the full effect of the smile he had aimed at her. Something inside her flip-flopped dangerously. Dozens of thoughts spilled through her mind, each of them scrambling to make themselves heard.

Jennifer knew darn well that the best way to a single mother's heart was through her child. How many men, she wondered, had gotten close to a kid in order to win over her mom? Certainly more than a few had tried with her. But she wasn't that easily fooled. Or charmed. Just as she'd seen through them, she was able to see that this man wasn't playing that game.

He genuinely cared about Sarah. It was in his every touch. His every smile. And her daughter was crazy about him in return.

Which only made this situation even more risky. Sarah loved him. That meant that he was already an accepted part of the little girl's life. And that, in turn, meant that he would be missed when he left. And he *would* leave.

Jennifer's heart did that weird little hip-hop again and she wished she could just for a moment reach in and still it. Didn't that flighty organ realize that caring about Chance Barnett Connelly was only asking for trouble?

"What are you thinking?" he asked, and she blinked, drawing herself out of the jumble of thoughts to face the predicament staring right at her.

She took a long, deep breath hoping to steady her voice, then said, "I'm thinking we should get out of this room before we wake her up." Giving Sarah one last glance, Jennifer turned and led the way out of the baby's room and didn't stop walking until she was in the center of the living room. Here, at least, there were bright lights and the radio crackling with the sounds of sixties' rock and roll. There were no patches of soft light, no need for whispers, no need to stand close together in the darkness.

Running her hands up and down her forearms,

she told herself that was a good thing. Too bad her body wasn't listening.

Chance walked directly to her and stopped just an inch or so short of actually touching her. Everything in her ached for him to reach out, grab hold of her and pull her into his arms—so to be sure that didn't happen, she backed up just a step.

"Are you all right?" he asked.

Concern rang true in his voice and she wanted to say, Heck no, I'm not all right. I'm scared. And lonely. And hungry for you. But she didn't. She couldn't.

"I'm fine," she finally managed to squeeze past the knot in her throat. "Just tired. That's all."

"And worried."

She sighed. "That, too."

"What time tomorrow does Sarah have to be at the hospital?"

Oh, God. Desire withered in the space of a heartbeat and was completely swallowed by fear.

"Ten."

"I'll be here at nine."

Her gaze shot to his. She read his determination in his whiskey-colored eyes and knew even before she started arguing with him that she would lose. "You don't have to do that."

"I didn't say I *had* to," he said softly. "I said I'd be here."

And she knew he would be. If there was one

thing she'd learned in the last week and a half, it was that when Chance gave his word, he didn't break it.

"I should try to talk you out of this," she heard herself say. "But I'm not going to."

"Good," he said and flashed his grin at her. "You'd lose."

"There is that," she admitted, since he was a pretty formidable foe. After all, she still had that swing set in her backyard, didn't she? "But that's not the only reason."

"Yeah?"

"Yeah." Okay, so she wasn't ready to admit that she wanted him as badly as a teenager feeling her first blast of hormones. But she could at least be partially honest. "I don't think I could stand taking her in by myself. I mean, I *could* take her, but then I'd be alone while they were getting her ready for—" Suddenly she didn't even want to use the word *operation*. Didn't even want to think about a team of doctors and nurses hovering over her baby's inert body.

Jennifer's eyes squeezed shut, blocking out the mental images that were always too near lately. And when she felt Chance's arms come around her, she simply leaned into his strength, giving quiet thanks that he was there.

"You don't have to be alone," he told her, and

she felt the brush of his breath across the top of her head.

His heartbeat hammered beneath her ear and she clung to the steady, sure beat of it. "I know. Thank you."

He pulled back a bit and when she looked up at him, she saw the slight frown tugging at his lips. "You don't need to thank me for being here for you, Jennifer."

"But—"

"I'm not here as a favor."

"I know that," she said, and swallowed hard. Staring up into his eyes, she watched desire, hunger and compassion flit across their surface and her insides twisted. "I really do know that."

He nodded slowly, keeping his gaze locked with hers. "Good. Because the only reason I'm here with you is because here is where I want to be."

"I'm glad," she said, needing to let him know just what his presence meant to her. She hadn't expected to care about him. Hadn't wanted to care about him. But those feelings were there. She could keep them a secret from him, but there was absolutely no point in trying to pretend to herself.

One corner of his mouth twitched up into a mere shadow of the full glory that was his high-voltage grin—and even that was enough to set off fireworks inside her.

He gave her a hard, tight hug, then let her go

before she could do something stupid like ask him to keep holding her. Good heavens what was happening to her?

For days she'd struggled successfully against these feelings, and now she was suddenly just a passenger on a hormone-driven train running out of control.

Reaching out, he trailed his fingertips down the side of her cheek, then let his hand fall to his side. "Try to get some sleep tonight, okay?"

She nodded.

"I'll see you in the morning."

She nodded again, her throat way too tight for words to slip past. So, in silence, she watched him walk across the room, open the front door and step out, closing it behind him.

Sleep? No way. There wouldn't be any sleep tonight. And it wasn't just fear for Sarah that would keep her wide-awake for hours. It was the desire pumping through her system and the knowledge that tomorrow she'd be with him again. Things were only going to get worse.

"Please try to relax, Mrs. Anderson," the doctor said in his most practiced, kind-to-the-family tone. "I have every expectation that the operation will go smoothly."

Smoothly.

Jennifer wrapped her arms around her middle and

tried to ease the chills that snaked through her bloodstream. But nothing helped. Knowing that her baby would, in just a few hours, be lying on an operating table was enough to give her bone-deep shakes.

"Can I see her again?" she asked and hated that her voice sounded so small and tinny.

The gray-haired doctor with the gentle eyes glanced from her to Chance and back again before he said, "I don't think that's a good idea." When Jennifer would have argued, he interrupted her neatly. "Sarah's being prepped for surgery and it's best if you just leave her with us until after it's over."

Over. An ugly, final word, Jennifer thought, shifting her gaze to the mint-green walls. Why mint green? she wondered absently. She'd always hated the color, and had come to loathe it during the time she'd spent in this hospital as Mike lay dying.

Oh God, *dying.*

She shivered and gulped in a breath.

"How long?" she blurted. "How long will the operation take?"

"Hard to say," Dr. Miller said. "Anywhere from two to six hours, usually."

Usually.

Another doctor's words swam to the surface of her memory and rattled around in her brain. *Just a cookie-cutter operation.* But there was nothing "usual" about this. Her baby was going into an operating room.

Jennifer's stomach pitched suddenly and she clenched her teeth together.

"Thank you, Doctor," Chance said into the silence and stepped up beside Jennifer, dropping one arm around her shoulder and pulling her up tight against him.

Grateful for his support, she leaned into him, and instead of worrying about her knees folding, forced herself to breathe and concentrate on the doctor's words.

"Just try to relax," Dr. Miller said, then winced as if he knew just how ridiculous that advice sounded. "I'll be out to see you as soon as we're finished."

"We'll be here," Chance assured him as the doctor turned and headed for a set of double doors behind which lay Sarah and operating rooms and too many other hazards to think about.

Chance kept one arm around Jennifer and guided her down a short hallway that smelled of antiseptic and fear and into a small waiting room.

A TV perched black and silent on a shelf in the corner of the room. Vinyl couches in appalling shades of orange and green dotted the linoleum floor. Scarred but clean tables held a scattering of magazines and newspapers and a coffee-and-tea-vending machine stood guard near the door. On the far wall, windows and a glass door looked out onto a small plant-filled patio.

He sat her down on the couch nearest the patio and took a seat beside her. They'd already spent hours here at the hospital. His gaze shot to the clock on the wall. One-fifteen. And there were still hours left to go.

Suddenly antsy, he stood up and shoved his hands into his jeans' pockets, looking for change. "Would you like some coffee? Tea?"

She looked up at him, and a cold, hard fist closed around his heart. Her eyes looked battered, terrified. And everything inside him wanted to help...*somehow*. Damn it. There had to be something he could do. At least when he was out on a mission, there were weapons to check and stow, battle plans to be made. Here, he was as useless as the outdated magazines.

"No," she said softly, her gaze sliding toward the doorway that led back to those double doors. "I don't think I could swallow anything."

"I know what you mean," he said and took a seat beside her again. "But we've got a long wait ahead of us."

She sat up straighter and stared directly into his eyes. "Oh, I'm sorry. You've already been here so long. You don't have to stay."

Chance sighed and ran one hand across the top of his head. "That's not what I meant. And I'm not going anywhere. Not till I know that you and Sarah are both fine."

She folded her hands together and twisted her fingers back and forth nervously until he laid his hand atop hers. "Good," she said, letting her gaze dip briefly before meeting his again. "I'm glad you're staying. I really don't want to be alone right now."

"You won't be," he said simply, sitting back and pulling her up close. Her arms slid around his middle, her head rested on his chest and it felt...right. Resting his head on the back of the couch, he closed his eyes and thought about the last time they'd seen Sarah. An IV dripping into her arm, her little eyes swollen from crying, she had looked entirely too small to be in that big bed.

But more than the misery of seeing Sarah lying there so helpless was the pain of having to watch Jennifer's terror for her child. He'd wanted nothing more than to ease that pain. To be the one she turned to. To be the one man who could hold her and help her through the worst moment in her life.

And that feeling had completely rocked him.

Opening his eyes, Chance stared up at the acoustical ceiling tiles. He'd never before wanted to be that important to anyone. He'd always prided himself on getting in and getting out. For years he'd kept his relationships shallow enough to make a puddle look deep. He'd figured it was safest that way. He wasn't like Douglas. He'd never wanted an ordinary existence.

He'd never wanted to matter.

To anyone.

And now that felt like the most important thing in the world.

Eight

An hour later, they sat opposite each other in the crowded cafeteria. Jennifer didn't feel like eating, but to placate Chance, she'd agreed to come downstairs and stare at a plate of very unappetizing food.

"You can't eat it through osmosis," he replied. "You'll actually have to put the food in your mouth and chew it."

Sighing, Jennifer dutifully picked up her fork and pushed a series of straight lines through her scoop of mashed potatoes. Then she quit trying altogether and laid the fork down again. Shaking her head, she looked at him and said, "I just can't. I'm sorry."

He nodded and gave her a long, understanding

look. "It's okay. Maybe later." Then he reached across the small table and moved the cup of hot tea closer to her right hand. "But at least drink this."

As a compromise, she took a long swallow, but knew she couldn't drink any more. Her stomach was tied up in knots. There was just no way to put anything in there and not have it turn into an acid bath.

Sitting back in her chair, Jennifer let her gaze drift around the crowded eating area. Doctors, nurses and other hospital personnel sat apart from everyone else. At a long row of tables, they laughed and talked and, in general, looked to be having a great time. To them, this place was just a job. Where they reported daily to work. Where they treated patients and handed out medications and still were able to remain distanced from the lives of the people they touched.

Quite a difference from the rest of the people clustered around the tables. Conversations were muted, strained whispers scraped the air and were interrupted occasionally by a choked-off sob or quiet weeping. Jennifer looked at her fellow prisoners and, noting the desperation in some of their eyes, realized she too looked haunted. By old fears? By new ones?

"What are you thinking?"

She shifted her gaze back to Chance with relief.

"I was...remembering the last time I was in this room."

"Tell me," he said simply.

Maybe he was just trying to get her to talk. To ease the slow passage of time. But whatever the reason, she went along.

"It was almost two years ago," she said and in her mind's eye saw it all again—only this time, she was an observer. "An officer had come by the house to tell me Mike had been shot. They brought me here, sat me down, gave me coffee and told me everything was being done." She could still feel the sympathetic glances thrown her way from the dozens of police officers lining the hallways as they waited for news about Mike's condition.

The police department really was a community. Not unlike the military, she supposed. When one of their number was hurt, the rest of them circled the wagons and did what had to be done.

She fiddled with the handle of her teacup and fixed her gaze on her fingers as she continued. "It was nearly an hour before one of the doctors came in." The memory took a hard jab at her heart and she winced with the remembered pain. "I knew even before he said anything." Her gaze lifted to Chance's again. "It was in his eyes. Grief, pity. He said he was sorry, but that there was simply nothing anyone could do."

Chance reached across the table to take her hand.

She held on to him tightly as if readying to take the big dip on a major roller coaster.

"They took me to him then," she said. "He was lying on a bed, still hooked up to a few machines that beeped along with his heart rate." She paused, then said, "He looked so tired. I even remember thinking that maybe all he needed was some rest."

Chance squeezed her hand.

She laughed shortly, but there was no matching spark of humor in her eyes. "I sat with him and stared at the green walls and counted the beeps and held his hand and told him that I would tell his baby about him." Still holding on to his hand, she sucked in a deep gulp of air and said, "There were two hundred and twenty-six beeps and then he died."

"I'm sorry."

"You have no reason to be sorry," she said, shaking her head gently. "It wasn't your fault."

"I know."

"It was Mike's fault."

"What?"

She saw surprise flicker in his eyes. Pulling her hand free of his, she folded her arms across her chest in an instinctively defensive posture. "Mike loved his job. He loved the rush of danger," she said, and couldn't completely hide the bitter tinge to her voice. "He wouldn't—or *couldn't*—give it up. Not even when I became pregnant and I asked him to. I never understood that about him. I still don't.''

"I do," Chance said softly. "When the stakes are high, you're living life to the fullest." Shaking his head, he went on in a whisper meant only for her ears. "You can't appreciate living until you've brushed up against death."

She sucked in a breath, leaned in toward him and said simply, "Bull." And before he could open his mouth to counter that, she went on in a rush of words fueled by her own panic. "You and Mike are so much alike, you could have been twins. And neither of you makes any sense at all." Her voice dropped a notch as she pointed out, "Sarah is upstairs in an operating room right now, 'brushing up against death' as you called it. Think she's appreciating life?"

"That's different and you know it," he said hotly. "She's a helpless child. I'm talking about men. Men who need to test themselves and stand up to a job that needs to be done. If I could change places with Sarah, I'd do it in a heartbeat." His hands curled into useless fists on the tabletop as he went on. "What I do—and what Mike did—they're necessary jobs. Jobs that mean something to thousands of people. Mike kept others safe at a risk to his own safety."

"And died for it."

"True," he said, "and you know damn well he didn't *plan* on that."

"Plan or not," she countered, "it happened. And he left me alone and pregnant." Old pain reared up and with it came an anger at Mike she had thought long dead. Her gaze lifted to the ceiling and the floors above, where her baby lay on an operating table. "And now I'm alone, waiting to hear if my daughter will live or die."

He reached across the table to touch her arm, still tightly folded over her chest. "You're not alone now, Jennifer."

Her gaze locked with his. A tendril of awareness scuttled through her and she fought it down. He was here, with her, true. But not for long. And she'd better remember that.

Jennifer pulled in a long, shaky breath and released it again before saying, "I appreciate you being here, don't get me wrong…"

"But…?" He prodded her to finish that statement.

"But," she said, "you'll be leaving soon."

His mouth tightened into a grim, straight line.

"You're not really a part of this," she added, not unkindly and still felt a stab of guilt when she watched regret flash across his eyes. "You'll be gone soon and I'll be alone again. The reality is, you're just like Mike. You're anxious to be off chasing risks—and in the end, life will go on as it has. Sarah and me against the world. Alone.''

With that, she jumped up, nearly overturning her chair as it scraped loudly over the scratched linoleum. She grabbed her purse and rushed for the doorway, never looking back. If she had, she would have seen Chance hot on her heels.

He caught up with her in the hallway, grabbing her upper arm and pulling her around to face him. A sheen of tears blurred her vision, but even with that, she had no trouble making out the fury on his features. Her heart hammered in her chest until she wouldn't have been surprised if it flew right through her ribcage.

His grip gentled, but was firm enough to tell her that he wasn't letting her go. ''Don't lump me in with your husband, Jen. I'm not him.''

''I know,'' she said, feeling her stomach jitter nervously. Oh, she knew darn well he wasn't Mike. Being this close to him, feeling his strength pouring into her, signaled a sweep of emotion that she'd never known before.

Jennifer had loved her husband. But it had been a comfortable, warm love. A straight road of affection and tenderness, with no highs or lows to interrupt the sameness.

When Chance touched her, fireworks went off in her bloodstream. Her emotions went on a swift, sure climb—but could plummet again at a moment's notice. Haze enveloped her brain and a pounding, throbbing need settled down low in her body, making her want and need things she knew she shouldn't.

No, he wasn't Mike.

He was far more dangerous.

"Just let me go," she said, though even she heard the unsure tone in her voice.

"Not yet," he told her and started for the elevator that would take them back to the third floor and the waiting room. Four other people joined them in the tiny cubicle, so neither of them spoke. Silence reigned until they'd reached their destination. Then Chance led her across the room and out onto the small patio. Only there did he finally release her.

Jennifer rubbed her arm, but could still feel the imprint of his fingers on her flesh. She looked up at him and watched a dizzying array of emotions chase each other across his face, until she wasn't sure what he was thinking, feeling.

Finally, though, he inhaled sharply and blurted, "I'm sorry. I didn't mean to upset you. Didn't want to give you more grief than you're already going through here today."

"I know."

"But, Jen," he went on as if she hadn't spoken, "don't confuse me with your late husband. We're two different men."

"Different," she said, "but so much alike."

"At least in one thing," he admitted, closing the space between them with a single, long step. "We both care for you."

Trouble, her mind screamed, but her body just plain wasn't listening.

He cupped her face in the palms of his hands and bent his head to hers. She stared up at him, like a deer caught in the headlights, and tried to brace herself. But she had no way of knowing what the impact of his mouth on hers would be like, so there was no way she could have prepared for the onslaught of sensations that slapped at her.

A simple, brief, almost tender kiss. Just a brush of his lips across hers.

And the ground rocked beneath her feet.

When he pulled his head back and looked at her, she saw the same dumbfounded expression on his face that she knew was on her own.

"Wow," he said on an exhale of breath.

"Yeah," she agreed and leaned into his strength, grateful for the arms that came around her and held her steady. There would be time enough later to worry about that kiss and what it signified.

For right now, it was enough to know she wasn't alone.

"What's taking so long?" she demanded on her five-hundredth trip around the waiting room. "It's four o'clock. Shouldn't they be finished by now?''

Jennifer had nearly worn a path in the linoleum. She was making Chance tired just watching her. He understood the nervous energy, but he didn't like the wild look in her eyes. Or the pallor of her skin.

Standing up, he crossed to her and ignored the older couple sitting on one of the other couches. They'd been here for less than an hour and hadn't started getting impatient yet. Their time would come, he knew.

But for now he took hold of Jennifer's arm and steered her toward the glass door and the patio beyond. ''Come on,'' he said. ''Let's get some fresh air.''

She threw a glance at the doorway behind them. ''But if the doctor comes in—''

''He'll see us through the glass.''

''Okay,'' she muttered, swiping one hand through her hair.

He opened the door and instantly a blast of cold, fresh wind slapped at them. Jennifer tipped her face into it, closing her eyes and inhaling deeply. Chance simply stared at her, captured by the picture she made. Blond hair tossed and tousled by the wind, her arms folded across her breasts, her chin tilted defiantly up, as if she was somehow challenging the gods themselves.

And he knew he would always remember this

moment and just how beautiful she looked despite the fear crowding her.

"God," she said softly enough that the wind nearly devoured her words, "I needed to get out of that room."

She turned her head to look at him. "Thank you."

"My pleasure," he said and meant it. Damn, it was good just looking at her. Her navy-blue sweater hugged her curves and her faded, worn jeans clung to her legs like a lover's hands. And even now, in this tense situation, she made his body hard and hot and ready for action.

Of course, remembering that too brief kiss they'd shared a few hours ago only fed the fires within.

"I've been thanking you a lot lately, haven't I?" she asked.

"I don't know. Are you keeping score?"

"Maybe I should," she said, and moved toward a bench in the corner of the patio. Studying him, she continued, "You've been great, Chance. Really. But what I'm trying to figure out is why?"

"Why what?"

"Why are you here?" she asked, pushing her windblown hair back from her face with a careless stroke of her hand. "Why are you spending an entire day sitting in a hospital, keeping me company?"

"I already told you that. I'm here because I want

to be here." And in fact, he added silently, couldn't imagine being anywhere else.

She shook her head gently and said, "That's not telling me why, though, is it?"

"Does there have to be a reason?"

"Yeah," she said slowly, "I think there does."

He reached up and scraped one hand across the back of his neck. Uncomfortable thinking about— let alone *talking* about—his reasons, he managed to shift her attention just a bit. "Emma stopped by earlier. Grant was here, too. Why's it so unusual to you that *I'm* here?"

She stood up and walked to stand in front of him. Tipping her head back, she caught his gaze with hers and didn't let it go. Chance momentarily lost himself in the green of her eyes and thought that in another time, another place, he just might try to drown in the depths of those amazing eyes of hers.

"What's unusual is," she said, "I've known those people for a couple of years. And I know they care about me and Sarah. But still, they came, they visited and they left. You, though…I've known you less than two weeks and you've been right here beside me through most of this."

Because he hadn't wanted to leave her. Would have done anything he could to stay with her. But on the other hand, if she'd rather he were gone…if it would make this easier on her, then he'd leave. It'd kill him to go, but he would.

"If you don't want me here," Chance said softly, watching her eyes, looking for a sign, "just say so."

Jennifer laughed shortly. "That is *so* not what I'm saying."

"What exactly *are* you saying, then?" he asked, torn between irritation and frustration.

"I guess I'm saying thanks. Again."

"Well, stop," he told her, his gaze moving over her features with a hungry touch, "I don't want to be thanked. I just want to be here."

Jennifer nodded and gave him a long, thoughtful look. Something flickered in her eyes, but he wasn't sure just what it was. And before he could find out, her gaze shifted slightly to look behind him and her face paled. "The doctor," she said on a tight gasp and headed for the door.

The doctor grinned and Chance felt the weight of the world slide off his shoulders. He dropped one hand onto Jennifer's shoulder in support and listened.

"Everything went fine," Dr. Miller said, looking directly at Jennifer, willing her to relax, believe. "Sarah came through like a trouper."

"Really?" Jennifer asked breathlessly. "She's all right? We can see her?"

The doctor then glanced at Chance before shaking his head slightly. "Not yet. She'll be in recovery for a couple of hours, but once we get her settled into ICU, you can both visit for a few minutes."

"But she's fine," Jennifer repeated.

"She's fine," Dr. Miller said and reached out to give Jennifer's hand an understanding pat. "She'll be as good as new before you know it."

"Oh God," she whispered brokenly and lifted one hand to cover her mouth. "Oh, thank you, Doctor," she said and gave the man a fierce, hard hug that clearly surprised the hell out of him.

He patted her back awkwardly, sent Chance a sheepish smile then stepped back. "You're welcome. Now why don't you two go have some dinner and relax. I'll come get you when it's time to visit Sarah."

Then he left and Jennifer turned around to look up at Chance. "She's okay."

"She's okay," he repeated, knowing she needed to hear the words again and again.

"Good as new."

"Better," he told her firmly.

"My baby's all right," she whispered and threw herself at Chance, flinging her arms around his neck and holding on tight enough to cut off his air. But he didn't mind in the slightest.

"My baby's all right," she whispered, pulling her head back to look at him through teary eyes. "She really is. And it's over."

"It's over, Jen, and you made it," he said, lifting one hand to stroke his fingertips down her cheek.

"*We* made it," she corrected, then slanted her mouth across his in the kind of kiss he'd been dreaming about for days.

Nine

Lips, tongue, teeth, breath mingling, bodies touching; she gave him everything she had, everything she'd been holding back, everything she'd wanted to give since nearly the first minute she'd laid eyes on him. His hands moved up and down her back, scrubbing over her thick, cable-knit sweater until she swore she could feel the hard strength of his palms against her skin.

He devoured her, taking what she offered and returning it tenfold. He tasted of pulse-pounding excitement and dreams and soft whispers in the night. Her heartbeat thundered in her ears. Her stomach pitched and rolled. Her knees liquefied. She clung to him tightly, kneading her fingers into his shoulders, feeling the warm, solid strength of him surrounding her.

And when she finally broke the kiss and pulled her head back, she was struggling for air. She stared up into those whiskey eyes of his as her lungs heaved in breath after breath. Still dangling from his neck like an oversize pendant, Jennifer grinned up at him and said, "Now *that* was a wow."

"Honey," he murmured, "you ain't seen nothin' yet."

Something hot and rich and delicious coursed through her and she swallowed hard. Now that she'd kissed him, let him know just how badly she wanted him, there would be no going back. She knew that. She was counting on that.

Because now that she knew for sure that Sarah was going to be all right, Jennifer planned to take Emma's advice. She was going to grab a little something for herself in the middle of all of this. And if it hurt more when he left because of it, at least she would have the memory of being in his arms to hold on to.

"You're a man of your word, right?" she asked, letting go of his neck and dropping to her feet.

His eyes went dark and hungry. "Count on it."

"Oh, I am, Commander," she said. "I am." Then she snaked her arm through his and leaned into him. "But to make sure I'm at my best, I think I'd better eat something. Keep my strength up."

A slow, wicked smile curved his incredible mouth as he said, "Need strength, huh? Jen, I'm going to buy you the biggest steak in Chicago."

Two hours later, they were back from dinner standing in front of a familiar set of double doors. ICU.

Jennifer took a deep breath, steadied her nerves and held on tightly to Chance's hand. How odd, she thought absently, that two weeks ago she hadn't known he existed. And now she was hanging on to his hand for dear life. She couldn't even imagine having to go into that room alone.

For two years now, she'd dealt with everything life had thrown at her. She'd been strong for Sarah and had tried to be both mother and father to her baby. It hadn't been easy. In fact, she'd been so lonely at times, she'd have given anything just to hear the sound of another adult voice in the house.

Now, having Chance standing beside her, lending her his strength, giving his quiet support—well, it meant more than she could have said.

"Ready?" he asked quietly, giving her hand a squeeze.

Not quite trusting her voice, Jennifer nodded and moved forward when he opened the door and held it wide for her.

The first thing she noticed were the sounds. A respirator whooshed noisily. And a steady series of beeps shot straight to her soul, reminding her all too clearly of that last night with Mike. But this was different, she reminded herself as she forced her feet to walk to the side of Sarah's bed. These beeps measured the strong, sure beating of Sarah's healed heart.

Jennifer looked down at her baby and a choked-off sob caught in her throat. Lifting one hand, she reached across the metal bars separating her from her child and gently, carefully stroked Sarah's hair. She was sleeping. Sedated, the doctor had said, until she didn't need the respirator breathing for her anymore. There was a tube in her airway, feeding to the respirator, and two IV lines hooked to her small arm for feeding and medication and several other tubes and lines that Jennifer didn't even want to think about.

"Oh, baby," she whispered around a knot of tears filling her throat.

"It looks bad, I know," Chance said quietly, placing his hands on her shoulders. "But she's going to be fine. The surgery's over and now all she has to do is heal."

"She's so tiny. So very tiny," Jennifer said.

"But tough," he reminded her. "Like her mother."

Jennifer reached up and covered one of his hands

with hers. While they stood there in silence, a gray-haired nurse with sharp, kind eyes came in, smiled and busily checked the tubes and machines, read the chart, then said, "Just another minute or two, Mr. and Mrs. Anderson."

"Oh," Jennifer said, startled by the nurse's assumption, "we're not—"

"I know," the nurse said, "you're not ready to leave your daughter yet. But she's going to be sleeping for the next couple of days. She won't know you're here and you could both probably use some sleep."

"Thank you," Chance said, and Jennifer shot him a quick glance.

"I promise," the nurse assured them, "I'll take very good care of your little girl."

"I—we— Can we come back in the morning?"

"You can come back and see her whenever you want to, Mrs. Anderson," the nurse said, before leaving them alone in the room. "You're allowed ten minutes with her every hour."

When the other woman was gone, Chance smiled down at Jennifer. "Didn't want to correct her and start up a conversation," he said, explaining why he hadn't told the nurse who he was.

Jennifer nodded and turned back to Sarah. For the first time since coming into the room, she tried not to notice the tubes and machines and instead, concentrated on Sarah's face. There was a flush of pink color in her cheeks and the ever-present shadows beneath her eyes were almost gone.

She *was* healing. Relief rushed through Jennifer, making her almost light-headed with the force of it. She'd lived with the fear of Sarah's heart problem and now her baby was on the road to real health. A future. She would grow up and get married and have babies of her own.

And Jennifer's own heart swelled with gratitude and joy. Leaning over the bars, she planted a kiss on top of Sarah's head and whispered, "I love you, baby. Sleep tight."

"Champagne was an excellent idea, Commander," Jennifer said as she held her glass out for another refill.

"We're celebrating, aren't we?" he asked and set the bottle down after topping off his own glass.

"Oh God, yes, we are," she said, taking a sip and laughing as the bubbly froth slid down her throat. "I swear, I feel light as a feather. I mean, I know she still has to recover, but she's *going* to recover."

"Damn right she is," Chance agreed and felt the rich, full swell of pleasure fill him. The baby would be fine. Jennifer was happy. And, he thought with a smile, well on her way to being just a little tipsy. But hell, didn't she deserve to be? She'd lived with a suffocating fear for too long and now the worst was over.

Moonlight streamed in through the lace curtains hung at the windows. Music drifted from the stereo on the wall and soft pools of lamplight dotted the floor. Jennifer lounged back against the sofa cushions, watching him with a soft, secretive smile on her face.

"What is it?" he finally asked.

"Just thinking," she said as she stood up and set her glass of champagne down on the coffee table.

"Well, this could be dangerous, then," he muttered, only half kidding. "Usually when a woman says she's been thinking, a man ends up in trouble."

She shook her head and her blond hair fell in gentle waves about her face. "Not this time."

"Really?" he asked, standing perfectly still as she approached him. "And why's that?"

"Because," she said, staring up into his eyes, letting him see the full force of her desire, "I'm thinking about that date we made earlier tonight."

"Is that right?" Everything inside him went hot and still. He wanted her more than he'd ever wanted anything or anyone in his life. And yet...Chance sighed and said what he had to say if he was going to be able to look himself in the mirror. "Jen," he started, "you've had a lot of champagne and—"

"Not that much," she argued, smiling up at him.

"Enough that it might make a difference in any decisions you make in the next couple of minutes." Damn it.

"You're the real deal, aren't you?" she asked and took yet another step closer until all that was separating them was the slender cord of desire vibrating between them. "An officer and a gentleman. Just like the movie."

Uncomfortable with that comparison, he shrugged it off. "I just don't want to take advantage of you when you're in a vulnerable frame of mind."

Jennifer laughed, a low, deep, throaty sound that rippled through the air and danced along every one of his nerve endings.

"What's so funny?" he asked.

"You," she said, taking his left hand in her right and putting her left hand on his shoulder. "For heaven's sake Chance, *I'm* the one making advances here."

"Yeah," he said, through clenched teeth. "I noticed that."

"Good. I was afraid you weren't paying attention."

"Oh, you've got my attention, honey."

"And I intend to keep it."

"No problem," he assured her.

"Dance with me," she whispered, tipping her head back and smiling up at him.

He arched one eyebrow. This he hadn't expected. "You want to dance?"

"Yes, I want to dance. With you. Now."

"Yes, ma'am," he said and pulled her closer. He was all in favor of anything that would keep her in his arms. Holding her tightly to him, he felt the press of her breasts against his chest and the warm grip of her hand in his. Her breath puffed across the base of his neck, starting a small fire that erupted in his bloodstream and quickly spread, sending heat to parts of his body that didn't really need the encouragement.

"You feel so good," she whispered a moment later.

"Not half as good as you do, Jen."

"I like that."

"What?"

"When you call me Jen," she admitted. "No one else ever has."

Something shifted inside him. Maybe it was the old loneliness sliding out of its familiar spot. Maybe it was the wall he'd built around his heart beginning to crumble. All he could be sure of was that he'd never been happier than he was at this moment, dancing in the soft light with Jen. He released her hand long enough to tuck his fingers beneath her chin and tilt her face up to his. Meeting her sea-green eyes, he said, "I'm glad I'm the first."

Then, still keeping their gazes locked, as if looking away might mean his life, Chance lowered his head and slanted his mouth across hers. The kiss began slowly, tenuously, as they rediscovered the magic they'd found only hours ago.

Electricity sizzled between them.

Heat exploded.

Hearts pounded.

And in seconds the gentleness was gone, replaced by a driving need that eclipsed everything else.

He couldn't get enough of her. That one thought slammed into Chance's brain over and over again. He needed her as badly as he needed his next fevered gulp of air. No, more. He needed her more. Breathing would mean nothing if he didn't have her.

His hands swept down her back to the hem of her sweater and then beneath it and up, up along the column of her spine, his fingertips tracing patterns on her silky flesh. She shivered in his arms and that tender response pushed him further, higher. With one quick, practiced flick of his fingers, her bra came undone and his hands shifted to take advantage. He cupped her breasts in his palms, never taking his lips from hers, never ceasing the greedy plunder of her warm, sensuous mouth. He tasted her and while his tongue danced with hers, his thumbs circled her rigid nipples, drawing a moan from the back of her throat that instantly set his soul on fire.

Chance groaned, too, knowing that she was drawing everything from him. Feelings, desires, things he'd banked carefully for years were scuttling to the surface and there was nothing he could have done to stop them, even if he'd wanted to.

One corner of his mind still shouted at him to throw up his defenses. To batten down the hatches and prepare to be assaulted. But it was too late. The years he'd spent alone were forgotten in the rush of desire.

He pulled his head back and, gulping in air, looked down at her. Her eyes were closed, and her mouth opened on a sigh as his fingers tweaked her nipples, tugging gently at the sensitive flesh.

"Chance," she whispered, her fingers digging into his upper arms for support. "Chance, that feels so good. So…wonderful."

His throat tightened. Just watching the play of emotions dart across her features was enough to swamp him. He felt stronger, braver, more sure than he ever had been before. And at the same time, his knees were weak and everything inside him was humbled, just to be given the gift of touching her.

"There's more," he promised, his voice low and deep, scraping against his throat. "So much more."

"Yes," she said, her eyes fluttering open to look up at him. "Give me more. I want it all. Everything there is."

"Everything," he promised and dropped to his knees in front of her.

Caught by surprise, Jennifer swayed into him slightly and he shifted his hands to her waist, holding her until she found her footing again. When her hands came up to his shoulders, he let his fingers glide along the waistband of her jeans, dipping just beneath the worn denim to dust across her flesh. "So soft," he murmured, "so smooth."

Her quick intake of breath was the only response, but it was enough.

Chance unbuttoned her jeans, then slowly pulled the zipper down, revealing a tiny scrap of blueberry-colored silk panties. Blood rushed to his groin and a fog rose up in his brain. The haze dropped over his vision but he blinked it back, determined to see her.

She swayed again and he gripped her upper thighs before tipping his head back to look up at her.

"Chance?" she asked, a world of questions wrapped in only his name.

"I promised you everything," he reminded her. "And this is just the first step."

Her hips rocked as she moved unconsciously into his touch. "But I want to feel you inside me."

Heat.

Pure, hot as the sun, molten lava, heat poured

through him. He tightened his hold on her thighs. "Oh, you will, honey. We *both* will. Trust me."

She nodded and gave him a half smile that reached down inside him and quickly turned him inside out. "I do, you know," she whispered. "Trust you."

Chance groaned again, tore his gaze from hers and turned his attention back to that scrap of silk. He needed it off her. Needed to see beneath it. To the treasures beyond. To the very heart of her.

He gave one strong tug and her jeans slid down her legs, leaving her standing before him with nothing between him and heaven itself but that small triangle of blue silk.

She gasped and his hands slid up her thighs again, along the backs of her legs until he was cupping her bottom in his palms.

Jennifer held her breath as his incredibly strong hands squeezed her behind with tender firmness. She was caught. Imprisoned in his grip. And she loved it.

The feel of his hands on her. The whisper of his breath as his mouth neared her body. The tension in the room. The pounding of her own heart that nearly choked the last breath from her.

She tightened her hold on his shoulders and looked down, wanting to watch him take her. Needing to see this man touch her in the most intimate way imaginable. And she wanted to remember it all. Everything about this moment was now chiseled deep in her mind. Every time she entered this room she would recall this moment. She would be able to see him, kneeling in front of her. His mouth nearing her body. She would feel his hands on her backside. She would experience the nearly paralyzing sense of anticipation.

And she would want to feel it all again.

But tomorrow would take care of itself, she well knew. And all of the tomorrows after it were yet to be faced. For now, there was him. His touch. His scent. His—

She sucked in a deep breath as his mouth covered her. He hadn't bothered to pull her panties down, but was taking her right through the silk fabric. She felt his hot breath. Felt the gentle scrape of his teeth as he explored her body. Felt the strength of his fingertips as he held her tightly and pulled her even closer to him.

His tongue scraped across the silk, creating a sensation unlike anything she'd ever known before. Wet heat surrounded her, tempting her, toying with her. She rocked in his hands, moving closer, but he continued his teasing. Again and again, he licked the damn silk that kept her from feeling him completely.

"Chance..." she whispered, her fingers clutching at his shoulders. "Please..."

He pulled away from her long enough to say, ''Please what?''

Jennifer tossed her hair back out of her eyes, looked down at him and read the silent command in his amber gaze. He wanted her to say it. Wanted to hear her say how much she wanted it. How much she wanted *him*.

Body on fire, mind whirling, she gave him the absolute truth. ''I want you to taste me.''

Flames danced in his eyes, and, in the next heartbeat, he yanked her panties down and took her.

She gasped aloud and forced herself to keep her eyes open. She watched him take her. Watched his mouth claim her in a way that no one ever had before. His lips and tongue and teeth tortured her gently. He pushed her so high, she thought she would never be able to breathe again and she didn't care. All Jennifer wanted, all she could think about was his next intimate kiss. The next swipe of his tongue.

Her knees wobbled and she locked them, refusing to give in to any weakness that might deprive her of the rippling sensations already beginning to build within. His breath, hot and wild, brushed against her most sensitive flesh. He tasted and suckled and teased, and her world spun while fireworks exploded inside her, shattering what was left of her control, sending splinters of brilliant color flashing across her mind.

He shifted his grip on her and slipped one finger into her depths.

"Chance!" His name shot from her throat on a choked-off gasp.

He didn't answer. He only redoubled his efforts, using his tongue to send her higher, faster, further than she'd ever been before. He caressed her body from the inside as he tortured her on the outside and Jennifer wanted him never to stop.

If she could have found a way to spend the rest of her life like this, she would have signed up for it. But even as she thought it, she felt her muscles tighten, tingle, and knew her climax was near.

She rocked her hips, moving in closer. She shifted one hand to cup the back of his head, holding him to her, as if afraid he would stop and leave her unfulfilled.

When the first shattering wave of completion took her, she surrendered to it, gloried in it and knew she was safe in the circle of his arms.

Ten

Chance stood up, caught her as she leaned into him and swung her up into his arms. One-handed, he swept her jeans and panties off her legs and let them fall to the floor.

"Okay," she said on a sigh as she looked up at him, "was that SEAL training or just a natural gift? Because I'm here to tell you, I'm impressed."

He grinned, despite the fever raging in his bloodstream. Her eyes were glazed, her cheeks flushed and even in his arms, her body still trembled with the force of her release. And it wasn't nearly enough. Not even close.

"You think *that* was impressive?" he asked,

shaking his head. "I keep telling you, Jen, you ain't seen nothin' yet."

She reached up, entwined her arms around his neck and whispered, "Wa-hoo!"

"That's the spirit," he muttered and tightened his grip on her as he headed across the living room toward the hallway. He'd waited as long as he possibly could. He had to have her. Here. Now. Before he lost what was left of his mind.

"Uh-oh."

His steps faltered and he glanced down at her. "Uh-oh? Not exactly what a man wants to hear about now, Jen."

"I know," she said, tossing her hair back out of her face, "but better now than in a few minutes."

"Okay, you have my attention," he said, stepping into her bedroom and walking directly to her bed. His fingers stroked the soft skin of her thigh while he waited for whatever news was important enough to interrupt this.

And he hoped to hell she wasn't going to say something like she'd changed her mind. That piece of news might be just enough to kill him.

One of her hands slipped from his neck, and she trailed her fingertips down his shirtfront, and Chance swore he could feel her touch right through the fabric of his shirt. Oh yeah. If she'd changed her mind, he was a dead man.

"I don't have any, um..." She stopped, shifted

her gaze to one side and muttered thickly, "this is nuts. I can have sex and I can't say *condoms?*"

He threw his head back and let loose a short, sharp bark of relieved laughter. "That's it?" he asked. "That's the 'uh-oh'?"

"Isn't it enough?"

"You remember when we stopped on the way here to pick up the champagne?"

"Yeah…"

He shrugged. "I picked up a little something else, too."

"Really?" Her eyes widened.

"Oh yeah." Chance laid her down onto the bed, dug in his pocket for a small package and tossed it onto the nightstand, then stretched out alongside her.

"My hero." She turned her head to smile at him. "You're really something, aren't you?"

"I try."

"I didn't realize that 'Be prepared' was a SEAL motto."

"Hey," he said, pulling her closer, "I started out a Boy Scout."

Her hands skimmed down, to his waistband, then she grabbed his shirt and pulled it free of his pants. "Boy Scout, huh?" she said, sliding her hands up beneath the fabric to caress his skin, "then I guess that means you also know how to start fires?"

His smile widened as he gave in to the need pulsing within. With one hand, Chance caressed the length of her thigh, watched her shiver, then murmured, "And I won't even need two sticks."

She arched into him, lifting her leg to place it atop his. "No," she whispered, "you sure won't."

He took her mouth, plundering her, tasting her, their tongues mating in a tangled dance that tortured as well as pleased. Chance's hands scooped up the bottom of her sweater until he had to tear his mouth from hers long enough to rip it and her bra from her body.

Then finally, finally, she was naked to his gaze and he feasted on her. The lush curves and valleys, the smooth silkiness of her skin. His fingers moved to encircle her nipples and when her head tipped back into the mattress, he muffled a groan. So responsive. So eager for his touch. He dipped his head to claim first one rigid nipple and then the other. Back and forth, he divided his attentions, driving her higher and higher. He heard her soft, whispered gasps, felt her body tremble, delighted in the way she moved into him, silently offering more of herself. And he wanted it all. He wanted to bury himself within her, he wanted to feel her body welcome him, surround him and hold him captive for the next fifty years or so. He wanted—no, *needed* to be a part of her. To be linked so intimately that she would never be whole without him again.

As these thoughts and more raced through his

brain, Chance tried both to make sense of them and to ignore them. He'd never felt this before. This…connection. It was as if he could feel her pleasure as well as his own. She moved and it touched him. She whispered and his heart responded. She sighed and his soul went up in flames.

Too much, one corner of his mind shouted. Not enough came the answer.

It would never be enough. He knew it even as he pulled back from her, stood up and yanked his clothes off. He felt it in her hot gaze. Knew it in the rush of blood to his groin. Recognized it in his pounding heart. Eternity with this woman would never be enough. He felt as though he'd been waiting for this moment, this night, most of his life.

And now that it was here, he told himself as he covered her body with his own, he wasn't going to ruin it by thinking so damn much!

Her thighs parted as he came over her and he relished the welcome. He knelt between her legs, smoothing his hands up and down her body, exploring every inch of her, reveling in the soft, exquisite beauty of her skin.

She held up her arms toward him and breathlessly said, ''Be inside me, Chance. Be deep inside me.''

''That's just where I want to be, Jen,'' he told her and reached for the condoms. Tearing one free, he opened the foil envelope, rolled it on and then turned his attention back to her. His hands scooped down her body to the small triangle at the juncture of her thighs. Delicately, deliberately, he stroked her center and smiled when her hips lifted off the bed.

"Chance!"

"Let it come again, honey," he urged her.

"No," she said, tossing her head from side to side on the mattress. Breathlessly, she continued, "Not without you. This time it has to be with you."

He slipped one finger, then two, into her depths. The warm, damp heat of her nearly pushed him over the edge, but somehow he managed to hang on to his tattered and unraveling control. He wanted her in a frenzy. Wanted her desperate for completion. Wanted her to want him as badly as he did her.

Only then would he allow himself entry to her body.

Again and again he stroked her, caressed her, his thumb rubbing across the most sensitive spot on her body until she whimpered. She planted her feet. Her hips rocked into his touch. Her hands fisted in the coverlet. She bit down hard on her bottom lip and groaned as he quickened his gentle assault.

And when the first tremor began shaking through her, Chance pushed his body into hers. He felt her muscles clamp down around him, felt the contractions, felt her release quickening within her. And it almost undid him.

He moved, creating a rhythm that Jennifer instantly matched. Her fingers clawed at his back. Her heels ground into his waist. She cried out as the last of her climax crested, and a heartbeat later he followed after her, groaning her name as he found a peace he'd never known before.

An hour or two—or five, who was counting?—passed before Jennifer staggered from the bedroom. Every muscle in her body felt weak and soft and, she thought, extremely limber.

A smile curved her lips as she slapped one hand on the wall for support and kept walking toward the kitchen. In the living room, the lights were glowing softly and music still drifted from the stereo that had been set to repeat.

"Should turn those off," she muttered and thought about the few extra steps it would take to accomplish the task. "Nope," she decided, preferring to use what was left of her strength to get to the kitchen where she could find something to eat.

Chance was still sleeping, but who could blame him? After the third time they'd made love, he'd simply collapsed. Of course, so had she. It was only her growling stomach that had wakened her. And once it was fed, she'd stumble back into bed and cuddle up next to her incredibly talented lover.

"Lover?" she said the word out loud, trying it on for size, so to speak. But then, what else could she call him? He wasn't her boyfriend. Nor a fiancé. And he certainly wasn't a one-night stand. So, she told herself, *lover* was definitely the right word.

But how strange. She'd never thought of herself as the type of woman to take a lover. She'd always been the good girl. The obedient daughter. The loving wife. The dedicated mother. The brave widow.

Frowning at that thought, Jennifer hit the light switch over the oven, preferring its tiny bulb to a blast of overhead lighting that just might blind her at the moment. Brave. Hah. She hadn't been brave. It wasn't as if she'd had a choice. She'd simply done what she'd had to do.

Just as she had tonight.

Oh, she'd needed this night with Chance desperately. She knew darn well it wasn't going anywhere, but that didn't seem to matter. Tonight would be enough. She would make it be enough. And if her heart ached for him after he'd gone, then she'd salve it with the memories of this one incredible night.

She pulled the refrigerator door open, bent down and looked inside, as if waiting for an invisible hand to offer her something. Frigid air wafted across her naked body and she laughed to herself.

"Naked in the kitchen."

"Sounds good," Chance said from the doorway. "I'll have one of those."

She gasped and straightened up. "You scared me. I thought you were sleeping."

One dark eyebrow lifted. "I was resting my eyes."

She laughed. "Then you should have them checked, because your eyes snore."

He gave her a rueful half smile and reached up to shove one hand along the side of his head. Jennifer's gaze locked on to the play of muscles beneath his bare skin and something inside her went hot and achy.

Good heavens, she thought, surprised at herself. *Again?*

He must have seen the flash of desire in her eyes, because he walked toward her, leaned across the half door of the refrigerator and gently tweaked one of her nipples.

Her knees wobbled.

"I woke up and you were gone," he said, scraping the pad of his thumb across the tip of her nipple.

She swallowed hard, pulled in a shaky breath and managed to choke out a few words. "I was hungry."

"So'm I," he said, cupping her breast in the palm of one hand.

"Oh my," Jennifer whispered on a long exhale of breath.

He eased his way past the open refrigerator door and backed her up against the wall. His hands cupped her breasts, his fingers tugged and pulled at the tips of her nipples until Jennifer ached all over and felt as if her body was burning up from the inside out.

She flattened her palms against the wall behind her, instinctively looking for something to hold on to. Cold air sighed from the refrigerator and pooled around them, locking their heated bodies in a chilly grip.

"I want you again," Chance said, burying his face in the curve of her neck. His teeth nibbled at her flesh and goose bumps raced down her spine.

"I want you, too," Jennifer admitted as he straightened up to look down into her eyes. "What's happening to me? To us?"

"Who cares?" he asked, letting one hand slide down the length of her body to cup her hot center.

"Oooh, not me," she said. "Not at the moment, anyhow."

"That's my girl," he whispered and lifted her off her feet. Turning around, he sat her down onto the butcher-block cooking island in the middle of the room.

The cool, smooth wood felt weird against her behind, but Jennifer was beyond caring. All she knew was that she had to have him again. Had to feel him inside her. Needed to experience the wild rush of his body dancing within hers.

"Now, Chance," she whispered, grabbing his head and pulling him close enough to kiss. "Be a part of me now."

"Oh yeah," he muttered and kissed her, taking her mouth in a kiss that electrified her.

Parting her thighs, she took him inside her and wrapped her legs around his middle, holding him in place. He rocked against her and she arched forward, meeting his every thrust and countering it with one of her own. She'd never known such hunger before. Never known the need he instilled in her.

Heck, she'd never walked around naked in her own house before him. Now she couldn't imagine ever wearing clothes again—not if it would keep him from her.

Her arms went around his neck and she caressed his tongue with hers, gave him her breath, her soul, her heart. His rhythm set and familiar now, she moved with him as easily as though they'd been doing this for years. And when he clutched at her and spilled his body into hers, she held on tightly and rode the wave of pleasure that only Chance could create.

But a moment later, that mood was shattered by two little words.

"Uh-oh."

"That's my line," she whispered, leaning her forehead against his chin.

Chance lifted her chin with the tips of his fingers until she was staring up at him. "Where are we?" he asked gently.

She cleared her throat, blinked and gave a quick look around. "The kitchen?"

"Yeah. And where are the condoms?"

She thought about that for a long minute, then, "Uh-oh."

"Exactly." Chance disentangled himself from her and took a step back. Perfect Barnett, he told himself. Now that it's too late, keep your distance.

She scooted off the edge of the butcher-block island and reached out to close the refrigerator. "Well," she said in what he thought was a perfectly reasonable tone, considering the situation, "there's nothing to be done about it now, is there?"

"That's it?" he asked. Hell, any other woman he'd ever known would be either screaming at him or throwing something at his head. Something heavy and preferably sharp.

"What do you want me to do?" she asked, giving him a shrug. "Throw myself into a lake? Besides, you don't have to worry anyway. I started taking the pill six months ago to regulate my cycle. So, I'm safe." She looked at him, a silent question in her eyes. "As long as you're healthy."

"I am," he said quickly, at least wanting to ease her mind on that score.

She nodded. "Then there's no problem."

"But—" He shook his head. No way. No way did he deserve to be let off this easy. "Damn it, this was my fault. I should have kept my head. Should have been careful."

"We were careful," she told him, then gave him a brief, wry smile. "Well, mostly."

"I didn't say 'we,'" Chance said softly, "I said 'me.' I'm the one who should have been careful. I lost control. For the first time in memory, I lost control."

Jennifer inhaled sharply, let it out again and grabbed one of his hands. "You know, Commander, I think that may be one of the nicest things anyone's ever said to me."

"Most women would be yelling about now, you realize that, right?"

She shrugged bare shoulders. "I'm not most women."

"You got that right."

"And I'm just having too good a night to ruin it now."

She turned around then and walked to the counter. Lifting the top of the cookie jar, she reached inside, pulled out a chocolate-chip cookie and took a bite. After she chewed and swallowed, she said, "But since I'm safe and you're healthy, why stress about something that's over and done?"

"You're amazing," he said simply.

"Thanks," she said and took another bite. "Right now I feel pretty amazing."

He watched as her tongue swept crumbs off her bottom lip, and an instant ache of need splintered through him. Then she walked across the room again, opened the fridge and got out the milk.

Handing it to him, she dived back inside. "So? Are you hungry?" she asked. "Want to split a sandwich?"

"Sure," he muttered thickly, his gaze locked on the curve of her bare behind. Food was the furthest thing from his mind. Right now his brain was filled with jumbled images and thoughts.

He'd just dodged a bullet and he knew it. Thanks to birth control pills, he wasn't in imminent danger of becoming a father—so he should be happy.

The problem was, he wasn't. Well, not entirely. At any other time, with any other woman, he'd be doing a mental happy dance about now. But this was Jen. And a part of him he hadn't known existed before tonight was damned sorry he hadn't made her pregnant.

Eleven

The next week passed in a blur.

Jennifer had never been more grateful for an understanding employer. If she had worked for anyone besides Emma Connelly, she wouldn't have been able to spend nearly every waking minute at the hospital.

Of course, she told herself as she walked into the waiting room with two steaming cups of coffee, her gratitude wasn't limited to Emma. Her gaze went straight to Chance, sitting on one of the vinyl couches. Smiling, she silently admitted that no one had ever looked more out of place. His long, denim-clad legs stretched out in front of him and crossed

at the ankles, he had his brawny arms folded across
his chest and a thoughtful expression on his face as
he stared out the glass doors opposite him. He
looked too...powerful, too lean, mean and strong
to be locked up in this room. He had an air about
him that sang of danger and wild places.

A whirlpool opened up in her stomach, spinning,
churning, as she realized the truth in that thought.
He *was* danger. Somehow, over the last couple of
weeks, she'd been able to put that little slice of
reality out of her mind. But the truth was, Chance
was a temporary situation. Any day now he'd be
taking off, headed for God knew where—into
heaven knew what kind of risk.

Her fingers tightened around the paper cups until
she wouldn't have been surprised to find them
plunging right through the flimsy barrier into the
hot coffee. What had she been thinking? What had
she allowed to happen here?

And how would she ever be able to stand his
leaving?

He looked up, as if sensing the turmoil in her
mind, and his amber gaze locked with hers. Even
from a distance, she felt the slap of the heat simmering in those golden depths.

"Something wrong?" he asked, pushing himself
to his feet. "Is it Sarah?"

"No," she said quickly, wanting to assure him
that the baby was fine. They'd looked in on her only

a few minutes ago and she'd been sleeping in her hospital-issue crib.

"Good," he said, giving her the slow smile she'd come to know so well over the last couple of weeks. "I was worried that maybe they'd taken her back to ICU."

"Nope," she replied, forcing a light tone she didn't feel into her voice. "Doctor's orders still stand. She can go home tomorrow."

"Then why the long face?" he asked, taking the cup she offered him.

"Nothing." It was a lie. And a bad one, apparently. She saw it in his eyes. He didn't believe her.

He reached out and stroked her hair back from her face. He flicked a quick glance at the couple on the other side of the room, but they were fascinated with the news program playing on the television. Still, he kept his voice low when he spoke, so they wouldn't hear.

"There's something bothering you, Jen. Tell me."

She sucked in a long, shaky breath and blew it out again. Then shifting her gaze, she studied the oil slick on the surface of her coffee rather than look into his eyes. He was just too good at this. He'd worm it out of her and she wasn't ready to say what she was thinking. Might never be ready.

Heck, she'd just figured it out for herself: Somehow, she'd let Chance into her heart and now she had to find a way to get him out of it again.

"I'm just thinking about Sarah and how long it will take her to recover," she said softly. "That's all." And instantly guilt pooled inside her. What kind of rotten mother was she, to use her sick little girl as an excuse to her lover?

Oh, good grief, this has gotten way out of control.

"Hell, honey," he said, accepting this lie and pulling her up close to him, "the docs say that a few days' rest and she'll be better than new."

Jennifer latched on to that and clung to it as if it were a bobbing life preserver tossed into a raging sea. "It'll take longer than a few days," she said, more to herself than to him. She'd done plenty of thinking about this. She had to be careful with Sarah. Make sure the little girl didn't do too much, run too fast or play too hard. She didn't want Sarah taxing her new strength. Better to take it slow. Easy. Shaking her head, she said aloud, "She'll have to be careful."

"Well, sure," he replied, then paused for a sip of coffee. "No playing football for at least ten years."

She heard the amusement in his voice and bristled. "I mean it. This was a serious operation. She'll need time to recover. To heal."

He frowned down at her, concern sparkling in

those amazing eyes of his. "Honey, she's been healed by this operation."

"The problem's been *fixed*," she said. "But she hasn't healed. Not yet."

Chance watched Jennifer and wished he knew what she was thinking. In the last week they'd grown closer. At least, he'd felt that they had. Every day they spent together at the hospital, and every night they were together in her bed. He'd found something with Jennifer that he'd never thought to find. A connection. A sense of belonging that he hadn't known since he was a child.

For so long now, his only family had been Douglas. His one tie to the world. And it had always been enough. Until recently. Now, though, he knew he wanted more. He wanted to matter. To count for something beyond his job. He wanted to be an integral part of Jennifer's and Sarah's lives.

And as that thought struck home, he knew he needed them to want him, too.

Jennifer gave him a smile that looked too distracted to be real. There was something going on here that she wasn't talking about. Something beyond worries over Sarah.

And it bugged the hell out of him that she obviously didn't want to tell him about it.

"Jennifer?" A soft, female voice cut into his thoughts and he looked up as Tara Connelly Paige walked across the floor toward them.

"Tara," Jennifer said, holding out one hand toward the woman, "it's so nice of you to come by."

"Well," Tara said, nodding hello to Chance before returning her gaze to Jennifer, "I just wanted to bring a little gift for Sarah." She held out a small teddy bear in a ballerina tutu.

"She'll love it," Jennifer said. "Thank you."

"You're welcome. Hey, we single moms have to stick together, don't we?"

"You bet," Jennifer said, casting a glance at Chance.

Tara checked the elegant gold watch on her wrist and rolled her eyes as she said, "I can't stay. But I did want you to know we're all thinking of you. Especially me. I know just how hard it is to take care of your baby alone. To do all the worrying yourself."

"I know you do." Jennifer gave the woman's hand a squeeze. "And I appreciate it."

"Kiss Sarah for me, will you? Chance, good to see you again." Tara turned for the door, her high heels clicking against the linoleum. Glancing back over her shoulder, she promised, "I'll come to see you both at home in a couple of weeks."

"That'd be great." Jennifer watched the woman walk out the door and disappear around a corner.

"That was nice," Chance said and his deep rumble of a voice set her insides to shaking.

"Yes, it was."

"Are you sure you're all right?" he asked.

"Fine," she murmured, staring down at the ballerina bear in her hand. But she wasn't fine. There were too many thoughts racing around in her mind for that.

Single mom. Those two words had struck a chord that was still echoing deep inside her. She hadn't realized it until just now, but the truth of the matter was that she hadn't been truly on her own since Chance had blown into town—and into her life. For the past three weeks he'd always been there. For Jennifer *and* for Sarah.

Heck, her baby daughter prattled constantly about "Chanz," even referring to him occasionally as Daddy. An ache settled around Jennifer's heart as she silently admitted just how important Chance had become in their lives. And how big a hole he was going to leave behind when he left. As he would, any day now. His wound was almost healed. Pretty soon, he'd be heading out to put himself in the line of fire again.

Darn it, she hadn't asked for this. She didn't want to care for him. She didn't need this kind of pain again. She needed someone safe. Someone boring. Someone who would be home every evening at 5:15. She absolutely *didn't* need another warrior.

Her fingers curled into the bear's soft stuffed body. It was a shame, then, wasn't it, that it was the warrior she loved?

* * *

Two days later, Chance pulled into Jennifer's driveway and thought to himself how much it felt like coming home. A strange sensation for a man who hadn't known a real home since he was a kid.

Strange...but nice.

He threw the gearshift into Park, turned off the engine and set the parking brake. Then he just sat there. Staring at the house. Picturing Jennifer and Sarah inside. And imagining himself, thousands of miles away.

Scowling, he grabbed the steering wheel with both hands and squeezed until he wouldn't have been at all surprised to see the damn thing snap in two. It didn't help.

He was leaving. He had his orders. Just that morning he'd spoken to his commanding officer. In just a few short days, he'd be gone, headed back out into the unknown—and Jennifer and Sarah would continue their lives without him. In time he'd be nothing more than a pleasant memory. And not even that to Sarah. She was too young. She'd never remember him. Pain sliced at him. Chance tried to ignore it, but this ache went far deeper than a simple bullet wound.

This pain would follow him for the rest of his life. He knew it. And damned if he was going to allow that to happen. He wanted Jennifer. Needed her. And he knew damn well that she felt the same way.

Opening the car door, he stepped out, slammed it, then headed for the house like a man on a mission. Mentally, he started going over all of the arguments she might make and coming up with counterpoints for each one. This was the most important battle he would ever engage in and he was determined to win.

He knocked on the front door as a matter of courtesy, but didn't wait for an answer. Opening it, he stepped into the house that held so many of his hopes and dreams. Sunlight streamed through the curtain to lie in lacy patches on the floor. Warmth reached out for him and dragged him close. Closer than he'd ever been to such coziness.

"Daddy!"

Instantly, Chance's heart swelled. His gaze shot to the fresh-faced toddler already pushing herself up from the floor to run to him. He went down on his haunches, held out both arms toward her and grinned as she ran toward him eagerly.

"Sarah, no!" Jennifer's voice sliced into the happy moment and shut it down.

The little girl stopped in her tracks and, frowning, looked from Chance to her mother, standing in the hall doorway. Her tiny bottom lip poked out into a full-fledged pout. "Chanz here."

"I see that," Jennifer said quietly, "but you mustn't run, baby. Walk. Slowly."

Impatiently, Chance sucked in a breath and stood up. Walking to Sarah, he scooped her up in his arms and gave her a kiss on the cheek that stopped her pout from becoming tears.

But it didn't solve the problem. His gaze followed Jennifer as she moved closer, coming to take her daughter from him. Once in her arms, she ran her hands up and down Sarah's body as if assuring herself the child was uninjured. And a flash of worried irritation swept through him.

"Jen, you've got to stop this."

"What?" she asked, not even bothering to tear her gaze from Sarah's flushed face.

"The doctor says Sarah's fine, but you're acting as though she's at death's door."

Sea-green eyes flashed up at him. "She's just out of the hospital," she reminded him hotly.

"Yeah," he said, agreeing to a point. "And I know she's still recovering. But," he added, reaching out to stroke the tip of his finger along Sarah's chubby cheek, "she's feeling pretty good now. Yet every time she tries to show her independence a little, you stop her and wrap her up in cotton."

Jennifer's head snapped back and she stared at him open-mouthed.

While she was speechless, he pressed his advantage. "If you coddle her too much," he said, keeping his voice soft, understanding, "Sarah will never get to enjoy the freedom and health the operation was supposed to give back to her."

"You don't understand," Jennifer said, shaking her head and tightening her hold on the baby in her arms.

"Yeah, I do," he said and meant it. He knew exactly what she was so terrified of. He'd seen it in her eyes since the moment they'd met. The thought of losing the daughter she loved so much had her frozen in fear. Yet now, the danger was over. Sarah could grow up healthy. Strong.

But Jennifer wasn't seeing that. She saw only the danger, not the gift.

"You couldn't possibly understand," she said, and he focused on her instead of his rampaging thoughts. "You weren't here for those months when walking across the room made her so tired she was gasping for breath."

"No, but—"

"And I didn't see you sitting up beside her crib at night, watching her little chest. Waiting for the next breath." Her voice broke and it ripped a hole in his own heart. "Hoping it would come."

"Jen," he interrupted, prodded by the pain in her eyes.

"No. No, I listened to you, now it's your turn." Keeping her arms wrapped around her daughter, Jennifer said, "You can't know how I feel, Chance.

You don't know what it's been like, living with this. Sarah is *not* your child." She paused, lifted her chin and inhaled sharply. "You don't get a vote in this."

The baby hiccuped and gave a little half cry and Jennifer instantly started bouncing her up and down in a doomed attempt to calm her.

Stung to the core, Chance just looked at her. "No, you're right," he said softly, pushing the words past the knot in his throat. "She's not my daughter. But we—the three of us—have been through a lot together in the last few weeks." His back teeth ground together briefly. "And I thought we'd— Doesn't matter," he said after a second or two. She'd effectively pushed him out of their tight little circle, and that hurt more than he cared to admit, even to himself.

For damn sure he wasn't going to admit anything like that out loud to Jennifer. Still, there was more at stake here than his wounded feelings. There was Sarah's future to think about. And no matter what Jennifer thought, he loved that little girl, so he had to say something.

"Fine," he snapped, letting the pain inside flavor his words with a bite. "I'm not her father. But I love her as though she were mine. And I'm not going to stand by and watch you smother her without speaking up."

"*Smother* her?"

He heard the outrage in her voice, but he went right on. This was important and someone had to say it. "You can't protect Sarah forever, Jen. She has to run and fall. She has to scrape her knee and heal."

"Why?" she shot back, fury goading her words. "Why is it that you men think pain belongs in life? Why shouldn't I try to protect her from being hurt? Try to keep her safe?"

Frustrated, he argued, "If you wrap her up in velvet and tuck her away in a drawer somewhere, then she's not living. She's just existing. Is that all you want for her?"

Sarah's cries came in earnest now, but the two adults just talked right over them while Jennifer tried to soothe her.

"Living doesn't have to require taking chances," she said, shaking her head as she narrowed her gaze on him.

"Of course it does," he said, reaching out and grabbing hold of her shoulders. "Life *is* taking chances. Every morning when we wake up, we run the risk that this is it. This is the last day we get."

She blanched, but he plunged on. "That's life." Chance threw both hands high and let them slap back down against his thighs. "That's why it's so important how we spend each damn day. Bruises come with the territory. Everyone dies, Jen. It's how you live that counts."

Jennifer shook her head. She wouldn't listen. He could see it in her eyes. Frustration bubbled inside him. Hell, he hadn't come here to fight with her. He didn't want them squaring off against each other. Not when he had so little time left to be with her. Soon, he'd be back out in the field, and this cozy haven would be nothing but a memory.

And a sinking feeling in his guts told him that it was already sliding out of his reach.

"I want Sarah safe," Jennifer said tightly. "She's already run enough risks for a lifetime. She shouldn't have to know any more pain. Shouldn't have to grow up and be disappointed or hurt or left alone or..." Her voice trailed off into nothingness.

There it was, he thought. This was the real enemy he had to face. It wasn't worry for Sarah driving her. It was Jen trying to protect her heart. "This isn't just about the baby, is it?" he demanded, wanting the truth out where it could be faced—and conquered. "Who is it you're really trying to protect here? Sarah? Or yourself?"

Twelve

A deep, throbbing ache settled around her heart and pounded out a rhythm that ran in counterpoint to her heartbeat. It slammed home with the precision of a surgeon's scalpel and it was all Jennifer could do not to weep with the pain.

It didn't help to know that he was right about this, as he was about the rest of it. Logically, she knew she shouldn't treat Sarah as if she were made of glass. But she'd come too close to losing her. And now it was pure instinct to protect. Defend.

But it wasn't only Sarah she was bent on protecting. It was her own heart. If she allowed herself to love Chance and he were taken from her, it would destroy her. She'd lost Mike and survived, true. But what she felt for this man was so much more, it terrified her. And if she had to avoid crushing pain later by enduring slightly lesser pain now, then that was what she would do.

With that thought firmly in mind, she steeled herself and said, "You should go. Now."

"What?"

He looked incredulous, and she couldn't really blame him. This was coming out of nowhere, she knew. But it was better this way. For all of them.

She swallowed hard. "I mean it. Leave, Chance. Just go."

A harsh, humorless laugh shot from his throat. "You're kidding, right?"

"No," she said, shaking her head and holding on more tightly to the crying baby in her arms. "I'm not. I want you to leave."

"No way." He crossed both arms over his broad chest and planted his feet as if he was taking root. "Damn it, don't you see that this is the only thing to do?"

"What I see is that you're using the excuse of an argument to chase me off."

She winced but didn't admit to a thing. "Why are you making this harder than it has to be?"

"*I'm* not doing this, you are," he snapped.

Sarah's cries notched higher in volume and Jennifer swayed, trying unsuccessfully to soothe the baby even while her own heart was breaking. She looked up at Chance, knowing this could be the last time she would ever stare up into those whiskey-colored eyes. Her soul cringed away from that truth, like a child hiding from the encroaching darkness. But she didn't have a choice. These things had to be said. Better now than later.

"Look," she began, pitching her voice to carry over Sarah's cries, "we both knew this was coming. You don't belong here, Chance."

"*We,*" he said in a furious mutter, "belong *together.*"

Oh, God. Before she could do something really stupid like throw herself into his arms and beg him never to let go, Jennifer shook her head, tears and flying hair blinding her. "No, we don't. You're action-adventure man and I'm the home-and-hearth type. It would never work. This…thing we've shared was temporary. We both knew that."

Hurt flashed in his eyes and regret pooled in her stomach.

"Is that right? Funny, it didn't feel temporary to me," he said, and reached for her again, but she stepped back, determined to keep him at a distance. When he spoke again, anger colored his words. "Damn it, Jen, you're just ending it? Like this?"

Hot tears rolled down her cheeks as she whispered, "This is the only way it *could* end. Don't you understand?"

"No," he said tightly, shaking his head, "I don't. I don't get how one of the strongest women I've ever known can turn her back on something fantastic just because she's too afraid to take another chance on life."

She flinched as if he'd struck her.

"Don't do this, Jen."

"I have to," she said. "For all of our sakes."

"I *love* you, damn it."

He looked as surprised by the admission as she was. Her resolve wobbled along with her knees. She was loved. By a man she loved desperately.

And it changed nothing.

"Goodbye, Chance," she whispered.

His features closed up and for the first time since she'd known him, she saw him for the professional warrior he was. Hard and cold, even his amber eyes flashed out a warning. Hurt radiated from him and simmered in the anger rippling off him in waves.

He lifted one hand and gently stroked the back of Sarah's head before turning around as stiffly as if he were on a parade deck. Jennifer watched him march across the room. She watched the front door open, watched him step out and watched the door quietly close again behind him.

Then all she heard was the sound of her own tears and her daughter's tiny voice, calling for daddy.

* * *

Three days later, the silence in the house drove Jennifer back to the Connelly mansion. Back to work. She needed distraction. She needed to keep busy. She needed somehow to fill the empty hours that kept crawling past.

She felt as though she'd been through a wringer. Jennifer had cried until there were just no more tears inside her. And it hadn't helped. There was still an aching, open wound inside her heart and she knew without a doubt it would never heal. All she could hope for now was a return to normalcy. A return to what her life had been like before Chance had entered it.

Even though a world without Chance in it held absolutely no appeal.

She sighed, hitched Sarah a bit higher on her hip and told herself to be thankful for small favors. Like Emma telling her to bring Sarah to work with her, so she wouldn't worry. "We'll be fine, sweetie. You'll see."

"Chanz here?" Sarah turned her head back and forth, looking all over the empty hallway of the Connelly mansion.

Jennifer's gaze swept the place, too, even though she suspected Chance had left a few days ago. After the argument they'd had, she was sure he'd been more than eager to get the heck out of Dodge.

"No, baby." Jennifer shook her head and forced a smile she didn't feel. "Chance is gone."

Those three little words somehow sucked all the air out of the room, so Jennifer continued on, headed for Emma's office and her old, welcome routine.

Seth Connelly planted a kiss on Emma's forehead, then took a step back. He threw a quick glance and smile at Jennifer before turning back to the woman he considered his mother. "I'll call after I meet Angie."

"All right," Emma said, reaching up to put one hand on his cheek. "You be careful."

"I will," he said, adding uselessly, "don't worry."

With that, he turned and headed for the door, pausing only long enough to grin at Sarah. Then he stopped in the doorway, threw another smile at his mother and was gone.

Emma's own smile only drooped a little as she looked at Jennifer. "So," she said, "how's our Sarah?"

"Doing very well."

"Chanz gone?" Sarah asked, her mouth screwing up into a pout.

"Yes," Jennifer said.

"No," Emma corrected.

"He's not?" Stupid, stupid, she told herself as a white-hot flash of excitement streaked across her heart.

"Not yet," Emma told her, taking Sarah into her arms. "He leaves day after tomorrow."

The older woman watched her, and Jennifer wondered absently if Emma could actually see her heart break. He was still here. But he was going to leave. And he'd leave never knowing that she loved him.

A cold chill crawled up her spine and Jennifer wrapped her empty arms around her middle. Without even Sarah to hold on to, she felt completely alone. And the cold seeped into her bones where she knew instinctively it was going to stay.

"Oh, God," she whispered, and wished she knew what the right thing to do was.

"Jennifer," Emma said softly, "love is a rare and glorious thing. Trust me. I know." She smiled sadly and shook her head as she cradled Sarah close. "I've seen how Chance looks at you—and how you look at him."

"Emma—"

"Honey," the other woman interrupted her, "if you let this love that's between you get away, you will always regret it."

Regret. The word echoed inside her over and over again until it took on the rhythm of her own beating heart. She already had regrets. She regretted that she'd never told Chance that she loved him. She regretted that she'd been on the stupid birth control pills and hadn't conceived during that first magical night with him. She regretted that she'd sent him off to a dangerous job letting him think she didn't care.

And it would only get worse, she knew. Even as her breath strangled her, her mind filled with images of his face, his smile, his touch, his kiss. Each of these and more would haunt her for the rest of her life. And every time she dreamed about him, she would have to acknowledge that *she* was the one who'd ended it. That *she* was the one who hadn't had enough strength, courage, to grab what she wanted and hold on tight.

The coming years stretched out in front of her and all she could see was an empty black void. No laughter. No kisses. No shared secrets. No more babies. No arms holding her in the night.

"Oh my God," she said past the knot of emotion clogging her throat. "I'm so stupid."

"Not entirely, I'm happy to see," Emma said.

"Where is he?"

"He went to Navy Pier."

Jennifer grinned, leaned forward and smacked a kiss onto Sarah's cheek. "Watch her for me?"

"Sure," Emma called out as her secretary ran for the door. "But after you accept his proposal, you've got some calls to make about Daniel's coronation!" But Jennifer was already gone. Shaking her head, Emma looked down at the baby in her arms and said, "Would you like a cookie?"

* * *

At Navy Pier, Jennifer threw money at the cabdriver, yelled "Keep the change," and leaped from the taxi. The weekday crowds weren't too bad as she sprinted down the long boardwalk. It was still too early in the year for the legions of tourists that would soon be streaming up and down the promenade.

Her gaze constantly scanning the faces she ran past, Jennifer knew only that she had to find Chance. Had to convince him that she was sorry. That she'd been wrong. Had to tell him that she loved him.

A fierce wind raced across the surface of Lake Michigan and pushed at her, almost as if trying to slow her down. She shoved her hair out of her eyes and raked the crowd again, looking for that chiseled jaw, that short, brown hair and quick smile. Those amber eyes.

Music blasted down at her from overhead speakers and a clutch of school kids on a field trip headed toward the tours being given aboard a navy ship at the end of the pier. Kiosk salesmen hawked cotton candy, sodas and hot dogs and she ignored them all in her single-minded search.

And finally, she saw him. Stepping out of one of the shops, he turned his face up into the sunlight and Jennifer's heart soared.

"Chance!" She called his name and started running for him even before he turned, surprise etched on his features. She didn't give him time to think. She'd come this far, she wouldn't be stopped. Not when she'd finally figured it all out.

Throwing herself at him, she wrapped her arms around his neck and trusted him to hold on to her. He did. His arms snaked around her tightly and lifted her off the ground as she pressed her lips to his in a kiss designed to tell him what her fears had kept her from saying before.

Absently, Jennifer noted the smattering of applause her performance was drawing from the interested group of bystanders. But she didn't care. All that mattered was Chance. And being in his arms. Where she belonged.

At last, though, she broke the kiss and looked up into those eyes that held a promise of a future. And before he could ask the questions she knew were coming, she started talking, words jumbling over each other in her haste to be heard.

"I understand, Chance," she said, breathless, "I know what you were talking about the other day. Life. It's not worth living if you're not willing to risk everything."

"Jen—"

"No," she said quickly, shifting her grip on him so that she could cup his cheek, tenderly drawing the pad of her thumb across his skin. "No, let me say it. I *have* to say it."

He nodded.

"I love you, Chance Barnett Connelly." And once the words were out, she laughed, throwing her head back briefly and enjoying the pure pleasure sweeping through her. "I'm not afraid to say it anymore. I'm only afraid to live my life without you in it."

Around them, the crowd slowly grew as more and more people were drawn to the real-life drama playing out on Navy Pier.

"I finally get it," she said, willing him to believe, willing him to read the truth in her eyes. "Love. That's all that really matters. And if you're lucky enough to find it, you shouldn't be dumb enough to turn your back on it."

His arms tightened, but that was the only sign that he'd heard her. Seconds ticked past and Jennifer worried that she'd waited too long. That she'd missed the opportunity life had handed her because she'd been too afraid to grab it and hang on.

An ache settled in the pit of her stomach as Chance gingerly set her down onto her feet. When he let her go, she felt cold. And empty. But then he smiled and reached into his pants' pocket, pulling out a small emerald-green velvet box.

Jennifer's breath caught as she looked into his eyes and saw love shining back at her.

Chance felt as though someone had just lifted a three-ton weight off his back. "These last few days without you have been about the worst I can ever remember," he said and watched as a sheen of tears glistened in her eyes. He'd never been so glad to see anyone in his life. Hearing her call his name had sounded like the answer to a lonely man's prayer. "I'm not used to needing…well, *anyone*," he said and paused before adding, "but I need you, Jen. You and Sarah. And you should know that I was leaving here to go hunt you down."

"You were?" she asked and swiped away a single tear that rolled along her cheek.

"Damn right," he grumbled, remembering his plan for a siege of her heart. If he'd had to, he would have requested extra leave time, just so he could stay in Chicago long enough to convince her that she loved him. "I wasn't about to let you or *our* daughter get away from me."

She smiled and his heartbeat staggered. God, how had he ever lived this long without her?

"I want to be a part of your lives," he went on quickly, saying all the words he'd been rehearsing most of the morning. "I want to belong somewhere and I need that place to be with you."

"Oh, Chance, we do belong together. I was just too scared to admit that before." She lifted her chin and gave him a watery smile. "Well, I'm still scared. But I'd rather be scared *with* you, than *without* you."

He inhaled sharply, deeply and nodded. "Good.

Good. Jen, I can't promise to live forever—no one can—but I do promise I will *love* you forever.''

"I'll hold you to it," she warned.

"You do that."

"Oh, and there's one more thing," she said, oblivious to the now substantial group of people watching them.

"What's that?" he asked warily.

"More babies," she said. "I want more babies."

"Me, too, honey," he told her and gave her a quick, hard kiss that was powerful enough to curl her toes. "The more the merrier." Hell, he got hard just thinking about her belly round with his child. But first things first. Opening the small green box, he said, "There's just one more thing."

Jennifer stared down at the huge solitaire diamond winking at her and gasped. Taking advantage of her surprise, he dropped to one knee, took her left hand in his and said in a loud, proud voice, "Jennifer Anderson, I love you more than I ever thought it possible to love anyone. And if you'll marry me, I'll spend the rest of my life proving it to you."

"And I," Jennifer said, pulling him to his feet, "will spend the rest of my life thanking my lucky stars for sending you to me."

"So that's a yes?" he asked, one corner of his mouth twitching into a grin.

"Oh, you bet it's a yes," she said.

Chance slipped the ring on to her finger before she could change her mind and sealed its place with a kiss. Then he grabbed her tightly around the waist and swung her high into the air.

She grinned down at him, the cheers of the crowd ringing in her ears, and for the first time in far too long, Jennifer felt truly, magically, alive.

*   *   *   *   *

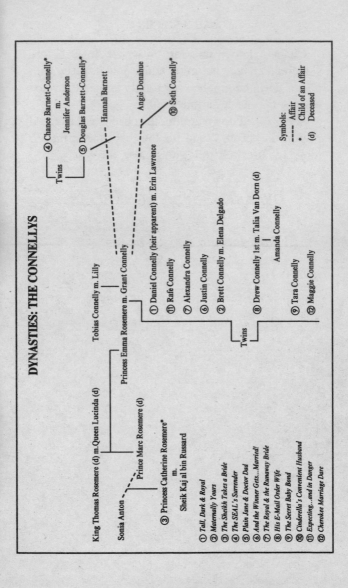

DYNASTIES: THE CONNELLYS

King Thomas Rosemere (d) m. Queen Lucinda (d)

Sonia Anton

Prince Marc Rosemere (d)

Tobias Connelly m. Lilly

Princess Emma Rosemere m. Grant Connelly

④ Chance Barnett-Connelly*
m.
Jennifer Anderson

⑤ Douglas Barnett-Connelly*

Hannah Barnett

Angie Donahue

Twins

③ Princess Catherine Rosemere*
m.
Sheik Kaj al bin Russard

① Daniel Connelly (heir apparent) m. Erin Lawrence

⑪ Rafe Connelly

⑦ Alexandra Connelly

⑥ Justin Connelly

② Brett Connelly m. Elena Delgado

⑧ Drew Connelly 1st m. Talia Van Dorn (d)

Amanda Connelly

⑨ Tara Connelly

⑫ Maggie Connelly

Twins

⑩ Seth Connelly*

Symbols:
- - - - Affair
* Child of an Affair
(d) Deceased

① Tall, Dark & Royal
② Maternally Yours
③ The Sheikh Takes a Bride
④ The SEAL's Surrender
⑤ Plain Jane & Doctor Dad
⑥ And the Winner Gets...Married!
⑦ The Royal & the Runaway Bride
⑧ His E-Mail Order Wife
⑨ The Secret Baby Bond
⑩ Cinderella's Convenient Husband
⑪ Expecting...and in Danger
⑫ Cherokee Marriage Dare

DYNASTIES: THE CONNELLYS
continues...

*Turn the page for a bonus look
at what's in store for you
in the next Connellys book
—only from Silhouette Desire:*

PLAIN JANE & DOCTOR DAD

*by Kate Little
May 2002*

One

As Maura Chambers left Scott Walker's office, she knew she'd never see him again. But he didn't say "Good luck" or even "Goodbye." He merely shuffled papers on his desk, ignoring her, as if she had already vanished from his sight.

She stepped into the busy hospital corridor, resisting the urge to give his door one last, resounding slam. What good would that do her now? It would only give the major-league gossips on staff more to talk about. Hadn't they already gotten enough mileage out of her failed romance? In a matter of days Scott would be gone for good, starting a new job and a new life hundreds of miles away. And she'd be free of him. Almost...

As much as she'd dreaded facing Scott again, she'd been obligated to disclose her secret. After all, he bore his fair share of responsibility. But it only took a moment for Maura to realize Scott didn't see the matter that way. His reaction had been more than disappointing. More than cold or unsympathetic. It had made her sick to her stomach.

Well, what did you *really* expect? She should've known, after the night Scott had announced he was leaving Chicago.

Looking back, it made her angry all over again to see his calculated tactics so clearly. How he had chosen a fancy restaurant for their talk, a place so formal he could almost be assured she wouldn't make a scene. As the maitre d' had led them to their secluded, candle-lit table, Maura had even thought Scott might be planning to propose.

He had a little speech planned for her—but it wasn't about marriage.

Getting to know her the past six months had been great, he'd said. But the problem was, he'd found a great job in Minnesota. Just what he'd been hoping for. She wouldn't want to hold him back, would she? Besides, they both knew this was a casual relationship.

Then he'd patted her hand. Long-distance things never seemed to work out, he'd added, so it was best for them both to end it now. To make a clean break. In a few weeks she'd thank him for making it so easy.

At that moment she finally saw Scott's true nature. How had she been so blind?

Maura felt her eyes tear at the memory. It seemed impossible that she had any tears left after the way she'd cried that night. She leaned against the wall and reached into her pocket for a tissue.

"Maura?" She felt a touch on her shoulder and turned to see Doug Connelly's tall, commanding form beside her. "Are you all right?" he asked kindly.

"Uh, sure. I've just got something in my eye," Maura mumbled.

"Here, let me see."

Before she could resist, he took her chin in his gentle grasp and turned her face up to the light.

His questioning gaze considered her troubled expression and she was sure he could see now that she'd lied to him.

"It looks as if it might be gone," he said quietly. His hand dropped away, but he continued to gaze down at her, his warm, amber eyes filled with concern.

"Why don't we get some fresh air? You look like you could use it." Doug took her arm without waiting for her reply.

Before Maura knew it, they were outside, walking down a tree-lined path. She glanced at Doug's rugged profile and tall, lean form. He walked with his hands dug into his lab coat, his ever-present stethoscope slung around his neck.

She had first come to know Doug as a colleague, then as a friend. While they weren't close, they'd always been able to talk to each other. Which was quite unusual for Maura. She had always been shy with men. Especially men this good-looking.

"Sit a minute," Doug said as they came to an empty bench. When they were settled, he asked, "What is it, Maura? I know you were crying back there. Is this about Scott?"

"No…not at all." She shook her head.

That's what everyone must think, she realized. That she was still pining for a man who had treated her so badly.

"He didn't deserve you." Doug's tone was firm and deep.

That struck her as odd, since Doug and Scott had once been close friends.

"That's nice of you to say," Maura replied quietly.

"I wasn't saying it to be nice. It's the truth." He paused, as if uncertain whether to continue. Then he said, "I know it feels awful right now. But give it time. Before you know it, you'll forget all about him."

She turned and glanced at Doug. The look in his eye, his expression of sheer kindness and consideration, was her undoing. She burst into tears.

Then all of a sudden, she felt Doug's strong arm

circle her shoulders and pull her closer, his grip strong and warm around her, his chest firm under her cheek.

"It's okay," she heard him murmur against her hair.

No, it's not okay, she wanted to say. It's anything but.

"Oh, Doug, I'm sorry...I just don't know what to do..." Her voice trailed off in another wave of tears.

She felt Doug's strong hand stroking her hair. She felt the warmth of his body and breathed in the scent of his skin. With her eyes closed, her cheek nestled in the crook of his shoulder, she felt so safe and protected. For the briefest moment, Maura allowed herself the lovely fantasy that she could stay this way forever. How much easier everything would seem, she thought wistfully.

But that was impossible. There was no one to help her out of this mess. Doug might offer his strong shoulder to cry on, but he didn't have a white charger standing by for a quick getaway.

She took a deep breath and forced herself to move away from his embrace.

"I'm sorry. I didn't mean to make you upset by talking about Scott," Doug apologized.

"It wasn't that." She wiped her eyes and took a shaky breath. She felt him watching her, waiting for her to speak.

Finally, she said, "It's just that I have this problem..." She paused and, staring straight ahead, added, "I'm pregnant."

She wasn't sure why she'd told him. The words spoken aloud sounded so final. So overwhelming.

Doug looked shocked for an instant, and was suddenly silent. His comforting, sympathetic expression grew harsher. Angrier.

"With Scott's child," he said. It was a statement, not a question.

Maura nodded reluctantly. But not before she noted that Doug's warm, amber eyes had mysteriously turned into cold, hard stone.

Silhouette *Desire*

presents

DYNASTIES:
THE
CONNELLYS

A brand-new miniseries about the Connellys of Chicago, a wealthy, powerful American family tied by blood to the royal family of the island kingdom of Altaria. They're wealthy, powerful and rocked by scandal, betrayal…and passion!

Look for a whole year of glamorous and utterly romantic tales in 2002:

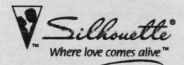

Silhouette®

Where love comes alive™

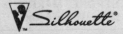

April 2002
MR. TEMPTATION
#1430 by Cait London

May 2002
HIS MAJESTY, M.D.
#1435 by Leanne Banks

June 2002
A COWBOY'S PURSUIT
#1441 by Anne McAllister

MAN OF THE MONTH

Where love comes alive™